MONTANA VENGEANCE

Ethan Todd, the crippled ex-sheriff of White Bluff, is free from prison after five years' incarceration — swearing vengeance on the Jackson clan, who sent him to jail and stole his star. When the White Bluff Cattleman's Bank is robbed by the Paulson gang, Sheriff Jeff Jackson pursues the fugitives, ordering a posse to follow him — but when the Paulsons encounter his cousin Sarah, they take her hostage. Will Jackson succeed in rescuing Sarah, and escaping unscathed from Ethan Todd's vengeance?

JAKE SHIPLEY

MONTANA VENGEANCE

Complete and Unabridged

LINFORD
Leicester

First published in Great Britain in 2014 by
Robert Hale Limited
London

First Linford Edition
published 2016
by arrangement with
Robert Hale Limited
London

A catalogue record for this book is available
from the British Library.

ISBN 978–1–4448–2718–7

Published by
F. A. Thorpe (Publishing)
Anstey, Leicestershire

Set by Words & Graphics Ltd.
Anstey, Leicestershire
Printed and bound in Great Britain by
T. J. International Ltd., Padstow, Cornwall

This book is printed on acid-free paper

1

A shack near Burke's Crossing

Ethan Todd lay back on the hard bunk; he'd plumped up the pillow but couldn't get comfortable. The constant throbbing ache in his foot was unbearable. He threw off the rough woollen blanket and looked down. How could his foot hurt so much? He had no foot! That bastard of a drunken French surgeon at the penitentiary had sliced it off. Gangrene, he had said. A second urgent operation followed soon after when the same doctor announced that the lower leg had now turned gangrenous, and it too had to come off if he wanted to live. Todd had almost died in that second operation.

He closed his eyes, reliving the screaming in his head; he had come round before the operation had been completed; there hadn't been sufficient supplies of anaesthetic. No one in authority seemed to react with any urgency, only a fast thinking orderly had produced a bottle of spirit alcohol. Todd remembered how he had guzzled it down eagerly; it hadn't helped much; however, the drunken state the spirit propelled him to was a thousand times better than the alternative. Nearly five years on, the grating feel and rasping sound of the surgeon's saw blade biting into his shinbone still hadn't left him.

He thumped his big fist hard down on to his knee in frustration as the horrors of that operation filtered through the barriers his mind had constructed — five years since they cut his leg and foot off — five long years of pain-filled hatred.

After his recovery, and it had been a long and pain-racked period of sleep deprived convalescence, Todd had sought out the surgeon, wanting more than anything to mutilate him as he had mutilated Todd, then to kill him slowly.

But fate had kicked Todd in the face once more: the surgeon had returned to France.

Todd thumped his knee repeatedly. What happy prospects did life hold for Ethan Todd now? Very few, he conceded. Not many people, if any, would employ a one-legged ex-convict.

Ethan Todd was still a proud man, a determined man. Now determined to wreak vengeance on all those who had caused his downfall.

I was a good sheriff, Todd told himself constantly, deliberately pushing all of his many misdemeanours from his memory.

Yes, he had been in the pay of the most powerful rancher in south-east Montana, but so what? Alexander Brown had been a generous employer; he had promised Todd a small spread, cattle and horses.

Todd had helped Brown's ranching empire grow steadily, and in return the big Scotsman had helped Todd live a happy and prosperous life. That was

3

until the Jackson clan and that drifter, Mike French had arrived on the scene. But for them, he and all of Brown's gun-hands would have ended up rich men.

Cheating the Jacksons out of a section of land abundant in high-grade silver ore would be easy. At any rate that was what Alexander Brown and his lawyer had said. Todd couldn't resist a rueful chuckle. Wasn't so simple in the end, was it? All his plans for a prosperous future were lost when Brown was killed.

Todd closed his eyes again, trying to shake his head free of the vivid images invading his mind, but it was no use; the unrelenting hatred burned deep and white hot. On that fateful day he and his posse of Brown's gunmen had ridden up to Jim Jackson's ranch, the Double-J, in the certain knowledge of their success. They had gone there to re-arrest the fugitive Mike French for the murders of Brown's foreman, Red West, and his gunman, the Lafayette

Kid. The hidden agenda had been to eliminate the entire Jackson clan, which the posse outgunned by at least two to one.

Events hadn't turned out as planned when the soldier boys rode in to spoil the party. Todd allowed himself another chuckle — that soldier boy, Lieutenant Hart, well, he'd got his just deserts: a stiletto, appropriately through the heart. Todd could still taste the delicious pleasure when he had buried the long blade into Hart's heart. He chuckled again, this time at the irony of the officer's name, for a brief moment forgetting his own pain. The surprised look on that soldier boy's face when Todd had twisted the blade deeper and deeper had been precious; a picture Todd never wanted to forget. What had been an accidental encounter with the young officer Todd now convinced himself he had planned and executed meticulously.

When the shooting had started at the Double-J the Jacksons got lucky. Brown was shot in the throat and died, along with Ray Cole, Roy Cole's older brother, and a couple of Brown's gunmen. Ethan Todd had been unhorsed and his right leg stomped on by his own horse.

It was he, Ethan Todd, who was jailed. It was he who lost his right foot and most of his leg, and it was the Jacksons who had done it: Jim Jackson and his three meddling nephews, not forgetting his two half-breed kids and his Crow Indian wife. A princess, they called Ika Jackson. Huh! Todd almost choked on the words. The daughter of a lousy Indian chief ain't no princess, he told himself. Anyways, he never did hold with whites marrying Injuns. 'Jackson spawn!' He spat out the words.

The Jacksons won the battle that day, but there was no way they would win the war. He, Ethan Todd, would see to that.

2

Bar-B Saloon, White Bluff, Montana.
1872

'Hey, old-timer, ain't you a bit long in the tooth to be out on your own?' Bobby Baston challenged loudly; his dark eyes were hooded, his words slurred.

The old man ignored the question, trying hard not to move a muscle despite his face and neck reddening. Most of the other drinkers hunkered their heads down, few wanting to make eye contact with the brash young man.

Bobby Baston wasn't a big man, nor was he overly tall at around five feet seven inches in his socks; he stood a couple of inches higher in his polished high-heel cowboy boots, but most townsfolk agreed he was a nasty piece of work. Most were scared of the slightly built youngster and steered a wide path around him whenever he was in town.

Bobby regarded his reflection in the huge gilded mirror behind the bar. He pulled his brand new dove-coloured Stetson hat low on his forehead to cover all but the back of his long, black slicked-back hair, fluffed up the collar on his chequered shirt, then drew a pinched finger and thumb across the brim of his hat as if to say, *Look at me.*

He swivelled on his heels, a grin on his mouth, but a sneer in his eyes. Bobby was evil personified. 'What *you* lookin' at?' Bobby demanded of another cowboy. The cowboy shrugged and returned to his drink.

Bobby turned back to his younger brother, raising his glass in a silent toast. 'Hey, barkeep,' he called out, 'let's have another bottle.'

The bartender's hand trembled as he reached for a bottle. 'Don't let's have any trouble, Bobby.'

'Not that cheap snake-oil,' Bobby

shouted. 'Give me some of that good stuff.' He turned to his brother, tottering against the bar. 'Bastard thought he was gonna palm that cheap stuff on us. Guess he don't know who I am.'

'Why don't you show him,' egged Sime Baston, pushing his hat to the back of his head. His grey-blue eyes gleamed with excitement. He shoved an unruly strand of corn-blond hair out of his eyes. 'Go on.'

Bobby turned back to the bar. 'Damned right, I will,' he said, his six-gun suddenly in his hand. He squinted carefully along the sight, then fired one shot. The bottle of red-eye in the bartender's hand shattered, showering him with glass and cheap whiskey.

'Whoopee!' Sime drew his six-gun, drew a bead on another bottle, and took a pot-shot. The bullet slammed into the wall a foot to the right of the target.

'Steady your arm on the bar,' yelled Bobby. 'Like this.' He squeezed off another shot, smashing the bottle to smithereens. 'OK? You try. Hit that bottle there.'

Sime rested his gun arm on the bar and squinted along the sight. This time the bottle smashed. 'This sure is fun,' he chortled, holstering his gun with a flourish.

An authoritative voice broke into the young men's laughter. 'Keep doing that and there'll be nothing left for you to drink.'

The brothers turned to face the voice.

'What's that, bub?' Bobby's eyesight was as blurred as his speech was slurred.

Lamplight reflected from the badge on the speaker's chest.

Sime grabbed his brother's arm. 'Maybe we should cool it a little.'

Bobby yanked his arm away. 'Ain't nobody tells Bobby Baston what to do.'

'But he's the sheriff.'

'Don't care if he's the Queen of Sheba.' Bobby tottered against the bar, putting out one hand for support; his six-gun in the other.

Sheriff Jeff Jackson extended his left hand. 'Mind handing me that Colt before somebody gets hurt?'

The youth eyed the sheriff belligerently. He took two unsteady steps towards the centre of the saloon and one back. He shook his head. 'What if I don't?'

'Then I'll have to take it,' Jeff said calmly, his commanding voice evenly pitched.

'Nobody's taking my gun.'

The words had hardly got out of Bobby's mouth when Deputy Ben North's shotgun creased the back of the young man's head. Bobby's body slumped to the sawdust-covered floor with a dull thud.

Jeff spoke first. 'You aiming to give us any trouble?'

Simon Baston looked down at his brother's prone body, then at the tall figure facing him. 'N-no, Sheriff.'

'Drop your gunbelt. Kick it over to

me then step away.'

The younger Baston brother did as the sheriff ordered.

'Hands behind you,' Ben ordered, getting the cuffs on him. 'Another happy Saturday evening in good old White Bluff,' he said ruefully.

'No real harm done.' Jeff grinned. 'Let's get these two miscreants squared away.'

Ben looked at the king-sized lump that was still rising on the back of Bobby's head. 'This one's gonna have one heck of a headache in the mornin'.' Taking the pail of water the barkeep handed him, Ben tipped half of the contents over the dazed youth.

'W-wha's'at?' Bobby spluttered, coming to in a hurry.

Ben pitched the rest of the water over Bobby's face. 'Help me get 'im up,' he said to the barkeep. The two men lifted Bobby to his unsteady feet.

Bobby spat out a mouthful of water, his face black as thunder. 'You'll be sorry you did that,' he said coldly, lurching towards Jeff.

'Put out your hands,' Jeff ordered, taking the handcuffs from the back of his belt.

As Bobby neared Jeff he couldn't resist the temptation to take a poke at the sheriff. Fortunately for Jeff the young man's movement was slow and predictable; he saw it coming and easily moved his head out of the path of the clenched fist. When it looked like Bobby was lining up a follow-up punch, Jeff stabbed out a hard left into Bobby's face, feeling the youth's nose crunch under his fist.

Blood spurted wildly as Bobby flew backwards across the sawdust-covered floor.

A couple of cowboys applauded. Another shouted, 'Well done, Sheriff. He's bin askin' for it.' One let out a loud whistle.

'Sorry, Jeff,' Ben apologized. 'Should've cuffed the sneaky little bastard.'

'Not your fault,' said Jeff. 'Anyway, it felt good,' he added in a hushed tone.

The unsympathetic barkeep threw a towel. Jeff caught it and threw it to Bobby. 'Hold that on your nose.'

All the way to the jail Bobby complained about the harsh treatment handed out to him, threatening Jeff with what his father would do in retribution.

After the prisoners had been safely locked away, and Doctor Hollis had bandaged Bobby's head and nose, Ben turned to Jeff. 'You expect any trouble once his pa learns what's happened?'

'Shouldn't think so,' replied Jeff. 'Why? You know something I don't?'

'No,' Ben answered. 'You met the major?'

'Yes. Seems a square-shooter.' Jeff looked at the clock. 'A reasonable sort of man. Union Army,' he added.

Ben smiled, 'Of course, you ain't biased at all are you, Captain?'

'It's sheriff to you, I'm not a captain any more,' Jeff joked.

'Well neither is the major a major. So what's the difference?'

'It's his choice. He can call himself what he likes. Either way he's a much better tenant of the Circle-B than the previous owner.'

'Alexander Brown?' Ben poured himself a coffee. 'Want one?' he asked. Jeff shook his head. 'Is it true what I heard happened?' Ben enquired.

'How the heck do I know what you've heard?'

Ben repeated the story of how the rancher and his lawyer had tried to cheat the Jacksons out of a section of their land where silver had been discovered. Ben was correct in most details.

'That's about it,' said Jeff. 'Maybe I will take a coffee.'

Ben sniffed the coffee pot. 'Think I'll brew up a new batch.' He screwed up his face. 'This smells awful.'

On reflection Jeff regretted hitting Bobby, knowing full well he could instead have caught the young man's swinging arm and twisted it round his back. He could have handcuffed him rather than cuffing him with his fist. Jeff rubbed his sore fist, recognizing that his over reaction had released a lot of the pent-up aggression that he felt towards the boy.

Bobby Baston had created a sequence of evil havoc ever since his father had purchased the Circle-B ranch. It was frustration that had caused Jeff to react to the kid's violence with excessive force.

Ben set down two cups. He guessed how Jeff must be feeling. For a long time he too had wanted to smack Bobby Baston around. 'You did the right thing,' he told his boss. 'Ain't nobody in town'll say any different.'

'Thanks,' Jeff said. Ben's words helped a little, but deep down he knew he had been wrong. Jeff looked at the clock again. 'Clay'll be here in a minute, so I'll leave you to it.'

'What about the coffee?'

'I'll get some at home.'

The door opened. Deputy Clay Boothe was early.

3

Double-J Ranch

Next day Jeff decided to swing round by the Double-J before visiting Major Baston at the Circle-B. The major's sons had been let out of jail and sent home with a warning. Jeff was determined to nip any potential trouble in the bud.

Dan Jackson was breaking-in a bronc, one arm high in the air for balance. Clem and Sanchez sat on the top pole of the corral fence. Clem raised a hand to his brother.

Jeff dismounted and tethered Atlas to the fence. He climbed up beside Dan's audience, Sanchez offered a broad grin.

'Where's Uncle Jim?' Jeff asked.

'Boulder Valley. Gone to look at a couple of sick cows,' said Clem. 'Should be back round lunchtime I guess.'

Dan looked over at his newly arrived cousin and shouted out a greeting, lost his balance and was unceremoniously bucked from the bronc's back. He hit the sandy earth with a thud. When they saw Dan wasn't moving, the three watchers leaped down from the fence and rushed into the corral. Sanchez grabbed the bronc's bridle and tried to calm the horse. Clem and Jeff knelt beside Dan's prone body; his right leg stuck out at a grotesque angle.

'Looks like it's busted pretty bad,' Sanchez opined, tying the bronc securely. 'I better go get the doc.' He dashed through the gate, cut out a horse, saddled up and sped away.

'Cheng,' Jeff shouted, 'get out here!' The Chinaman's face appeared at a window. 'Cheng,' Jeff repeated. 'We'll make a stretcher. Get him inside,' he said to Clem.

'You sure we should move him?'

Jeff eyed his younger brother. 'Can't leave him like this. Could be hours before Doc Hollis gets here. Assuming he's at home when Sanchez gets there,' he added. 'Cheng,' he shouted again.

Jeff disappeared into the barn, emerging a few minutes later with a couple of poles, two wooden slats, a length of rope, together with some cord and canvas. Cheng Li came out of the house to see what the shouting was all about.

'Leg broken good,' observed the Chinaman. 'What you do?'

'Gonna straighten it,' Clem announced.

Jeff laid the poles near Dan's unconscious body, looped the rope around the poles in a webbing pattern, tied off the ends securely, then laid the canvas across it; the project took only a few minutes. Next he gently eased one timber slat under the broken leg, laid the other on top and looped the cord around both to hold the leg steady.

Satisfied that the injured leg was supported securely, he said, 'Help me turn him over on to the stretcher. I'll hold the leg. Clem, you lift his shoulders. Cheng, you support Dan's other leg.' The others nodded. 'On the count of three,' said Jeff. 'One, two, three.'

Once Dan was on the stretcher Cheng Li touched Jeff's arm. 'Cheng Li do it,' he said shaking his head. 'Study Chinese medicine long time ago.'

The Chinaman looked and sounded confident, Jeff stepped away to give him room.

Cheng Li produced a long curved knife from his capacious sleeve, using it to cut away the timber slats, then the leg of Dan's jeans. Next he sliced through Dan's boot which he removed with minimum fuss.

'Dan ain't gonna like you cutting up his best working boots,' Clem told him.

Cheng Li ignored the comment and took hold of Dan's leg and foot. 'Hold him, please.'

When he was sure Clem and Jeff had a good hold of his patient Cheng Li pulled hard on Dan's leg. The leg clicked, bones scraped sickeningly against each other. Clem felt faint but held on tight. Cheng Li gently twisted and turned the limb to an answering groan from Dan.

He pushed hard, more clicks, then he nodded, satisfied with the results of his toil.

'Fixed,' he said simply. 'Now bandage. You wait, please.'

Cheng Li returned to the ranch house, emerging moments later carrying a white sheet which he slit into strips. He handed some to Clem. 'Hold please. Jeff, please support Dan leg.' Cheng Li applied the bandage, drawing the white cotton material tight. 'Now carry to house.'

Dan was stretchered to a bedroom and lifted on to the bed. Cheng went off to the kitchen muttering something neither Clem nor Jeff could understand. He returned with a glass and a jug from which he poured some liquid. 'Dan drink this now.'

Jeff raised Dan's head, Clem held Dan's nose, Cheng Li poured some of the liquid down Dan's throat. 'Sedative,' said Cheng Li. 'He sleep now.'

Later that afternoon Sanchez returned with Doctor Hollis. The doctor pronounced that Cheng Li's ministering was the finest he'd ever seen. 'Any time you want to give up cooking, you can come work with me,' he told Cheng Li.

Cheng Li smiled inscrutably.

A couple of hours before sunset the sound of riders coming at speed was heard.

Jeff and Clem rushed into the yard. Doctor Hollis and Cheng Li followed. Sanchez came out of the barn.

Two grim-faced cowboys reined in their mounts.

Jeff eyed the cowhands. 'What's happened?'

The lead rider stepped down from his horse, his gaunt expression concerned. 'It's Jim,' he answered sadly, 'an accident.' The cowboy took off his hat. 'Sorry', he said. 'Bob and Ken are bringing him in. Me'n Charlie came on ahead.'

'What are you saying?'

'Jim's dead.'

'No!' shouted Clem.

Jeff was dumbstruck.

A sad procession came slowly into

the yard, Bob Kempson leading Jim's horse; Jim's lifeless body was draped across the horse's back.

Doctor Hollis was first to react. 'What happened?'

Bob was obviously grieving. 'Gimme a minute, Doc.' He brushed away a tear as he and Ken lifted Jim's body from the horse's back.

'Bring him into the house,' said the doctor.

Clem and Jeff were still in shock.

Doctor Hollis examined Jim's body. He bowed his head solemnly.

Cheng Li made a hot sweet drink for everyone.

Bob Kempson composed himself. 'We was down by Pitcher's Creek. Jim thought he'd heard a yearling in distress an' rode up the small crest near that stand of firs, you know the one.' Everyone nodded. 'He'd looked at all the other sick cows, and was happy it weren't nothin' serious. Next thing you know I heard a commotion and turned to see his horse rearin' an' Jim fallin'.'

He paused to take a sip of his drink. 'By the time I reached him he was dead. There was blood oozin' out of a cut on his head an' lots of it on a big rock next to where I found him. Can't believe it,' he sobbed. 'Jim Jackson was the best boss I ever had. Took me in. Never asked nothin'.' Bob's tears overcame him.

'There was nothing you or anyone could have done, Bob,' comforted Doctor Hollis. He turned to look at Clem and Jeff; both had tears streaming down their faces. 'Where's Jim's wife? Where's Ika and the kids?' he asked nobody in particular. 'They need to be told.'

'I'll go,' volunteered Clem, feeling the need to do something to take his mind off what had happened. 'They went to see Red Hawk.'

'Must've been spooked by a rattler, I guess,' said Bob, regaining something of his composure.

4

The Baptist Church, White Bluff

The preacher introduced the closing hymn, and the pipe organ pumped out the introduction to *Nearer, My God to thee*, not Jeff's favourite. The congregation of the newly built church rose as one; a solemn cacophony of boots and shoes scraping on wooded floorboards. The crowded front pews were filled with Jacksons, many fidgeting with handkerchiefs.

The hymn book trembled in Jeff's hand. He couldn't sing, his throat was too tight and constricted by grief; instead he mouthed the words. Laurie rested her hand on his, the pressure of her fingers warm and comforting. He leaned towards his wife, needing to feel the pressure of her hip against his. He had always hated funerals, but this was far worse than any he had attended previously.

The little church was full; some people couldn't get in.

Standing at the front Jeff felt awkward. He felt every eye on him; he would have much preferred to be at the back, suddenly remembering that this wasn't about him. A tearful Ika stood straight-backed and proud, looking down at her husband's coffin in front of the altar, her eyes not leaving the place where her husband lay. She was flanked by Sarah and Jason, both good-looking kids, Jeff thought. Jeff knew Jason would hate wearing the suit Ika had insisted upon; the collar and tie were no doubt choking the life out of him. Jim's son was more Indian than white, loved hunting and riding with his Crow relatives and friends. Sarah was more white in her ways. A pretty girl who at fourteen, going on eighteen, was fast growing out of her tomboy ways. Lovely kids. All three were holding up well. Sarah comforted her mother, an arm around her waist, tears rolling down her cheeks, eyes red-rimmed.

The second verse started, the hymn threatening to go on for ever. Clem looked across at Jeff, his tear lined face looked drained. Dan stood next to his cousin leaning heavily on a crutch, staring straight ahead; neither wanted to look at the pine coffin resting on the trestles.

Jeff hadn't yet cried; however he knew the sadness would catch up with him sooner than later. His sorrow at not being able to say goodbye to Jim ate away at his insides, like a tiger tearing away the lining of his stomach. Their last words together had been some innocuous discussion about the weather.

A well worn 'Old Glory' was draped over the coffin. The flag had been supplied by Jeff's father-in-law, Lars Andersen.

Deep in his thoughts about Jim, Jeff hadn't noticed the hymn had at last ended. The preacher closed the big Bible with a bang, snapping Jeff back to the present. The congregation rose to their feet. An usher tapped Jeff's shoulder, gesturing for him to join Ika in leading the mourners from the church.

Jeff paced the tiny graveyard still in a semi-trance of misery. Already he felt Jim's loss acutely. What would life be like without him? For more than five years Jim had taken on the role of surrogate father to all three Jackson boys.

The coffin was loaded on to the hearse and the mourners headed for the Double-J, to the quiet spot down by the river that marked the graves of Jim's first wife and child, and that of Dan's second cousin, Billy Welch, who had been murdered by Alexander Brown's gunman, the Lafayette Kid.

Jeff was troubled by the circumstances of Jim's death; he was not altogether happy with Doctor Hollis's diagnosis. For an experienced rider to fall from horseback whilst the animal was static seemed unlikely, especially a skilled and proficient horseman like Jim Jackson. Something about his uncle's death didn't sit right. Jeff resolved to ride out to the spot to see for himself: to see what, he couldn't say. He hoped that taking a look around would either exorcise the nagging demons of doubt eating away at his insides or confirm his vague suspicions that Jim Jackson's death hadn't been an accident. Jeff didn't want to admit he was clutching at straws, but somehow he needed there to be a reason for Jim's death.

'Jeff,' Laurie called softly, snapping Jeff out of his mournful and suspicious thoughts. She picked up a handful of earth, Jeff did the same. 'Ashes to ashes,' they intoned, allowing the soft earth to fall from their hands. The preacher smiled benignly as he shook Jeff's hand.

* * *

The drive back to town was made in silence. One corner of the saloon had been hired for the funeral reception. From the pulpit the preacher had told the congregation everyone was welcome.

Laurie had organized a large ham, chicken, beef, and cheeses. A free bar was open for any wishing to partake of something stronger than coffee or tea.

'Coffee, or something stronger?' Clem asked Jeff.

'Coffee for me,' Jeff replied.

'Coffee it is.' Clem turned, 'Laurie?'

'I'll have coffee as well,' she answered. 'Get the children a sarsaparilla, will you?'

'Coming right up,' promised Clem. 'That table's reserved for family.' He pointed across the room, and walked towards the bar.

'Weren't no accident,' he heard a voice say.

His ears pricked up. He rounded on the man who had spoken the words. 'What'd you say?'

The man lurched against the bar, grabbing at the polished wooden surface for support. He eyed Clem through blood-shot eyes.

'Said it weren't no accident.' His words were slurred.

Clem let the man speak. He was smaller than average height, his waxen skin was like that of a corpse, his whiskers grey as was the shock of unkempt hair that spilled out from under his battered sweat-stained bowler hat; his clothes were dirty and well worn. He didn't smell too sweet. The man hiccuped, his rancid breath heavy with the smell of whiskey.

'Seen 'im. Didn't see me. But I seen him.'

Clem stepped backwards half a pace and fanned away the putrid air. 'What did you see?'

The man rolled his eyes, lurching forward. Clem pushed him back against the bar.

'What did you see?' Clem repeated.

The small man peered beyond his questioner through glazed eyes at some unknown object in the distance. His gaze swung back to Clem suddenly, as though the man was seeing him for the first time. 'Not me,' he gabbled out, 'I never did nothin'.'

Frustrated, Clem grabbed the front of the man's soiled shirt, pulling the man to him. 'I asked you what you saw.'

The man appeared oblivious to Clem's demands. He stared straight ahead, his eyes semi-vacant.

'Leave him,' Dan Jackson told his cousin. 'He's a few slates short of a full roof.'

Reluctantly Clem released his grip, allowing the man's heels to return to contact with the floor.

'Buy me a drink,' the man burped out.

'Drinks are free,' said Dan. 'What do you want?'

The man half-turned. 'Whiskey.'

'Take no notice of him, he's drunk,' the barkeep said, filling the man's tumbler.

'Know who he is, Sid?' asked Dan.

'Nope. Came in earlier. First time I seen 'im.'

Dan helped the staggering man to a chair, then returned to the bar. He laid his crutch on the polished surface and hoisted his busted leg on to the brass rail. 'What'd you make of what the little guy said?'

'Don't rightly know,' replied Clem, 'but I aim to find out when he sobers up.' He looked across at the little man; he was snoring loudly, head slumped on the table.

The saloon was full, all the talk was of Jim Jackson and his life. What a good citizen he had been. A shame he had died so young. Friends who, in life, Jim Jackson never knew he had, now praised him in death.

Clem tapped his cousin's arm. 'Where's Jeff? He was here a minute ago.'

Dan peered around the saloon. 'Can't see him.'

Clem swallowed a mouthful of whiskey. 'That feller knows something, I'm sure of it.'

Dan shook his head. 'Aw, he's just a drunken windbag.'

'No, Cousin. He knows something,' Clem said through gritted teeth, 'and I aim to get it out of him. In any case we need to tell Jeff what he said.'

Clem sought out his older brother,

finding him sitting with Laurie. He took Jeff to one side and told him what had happened. Jeff agreed: the man must be interrogated when he wasn't drunk.

Early next morning the two brothers found the little man in the saloon, moments before he could get a drink. They took him to Mrs O'Shaughnessy's café and plied him with coffee, but the little man said he didn't remember anything about the previous night, nor did he recall saying anything about Jim's death not being an accident. Claimed he'd never even heard of Jim Jackson.

★   ★   ★

Jeff dismounted slowly, loose-tethering Atlas to the limb of a tree. The big black horse began cropping at the sparse herbage. There wasn't much to see on the ridge. The hard earth was covered in a multitude of hoofprints. Many riders would have made for the spot once Bob had raised the alarm on seeing Jim go down. It had also rained since the accident.

Jeff stayed on the hill for almost thirty minutes, then returned to town, hitching his horse to the rail outside Laurie's father's store.

A wagon drew up. The driver got down from the seat, lifted a weight from the back and hooked it on to the nearest horse's bridle. He stepped up on to the stoop and reached for the handle of the general store's door. He saw Jeff and nodded a greeting as he entered.

'Sheriff. You hear what that little runt was saying yesterday?'

Jeff turned slowly to face the speaker with the drawling voice.

The man asking the question seemed friendly enough. He was missing a few front teeth, and was leaning back against a wall; the tilted wooden chair he sat on looked in danger of toppling over. A battered narrow-brimmed hat was pulled low over his eyes.

Jeff didn't recognize him. 'You new in town?' he asked.

The stranger spat out a stream of tobacco juice. 'Yep. Got in a coupla days ago.' He answered politely, his accent definitely Southern.

'What you asked before . . . ' Jeff paused. 'You speaking of Jim Jackson?'

'He was your uncle, weren't he?'

'My father's cousin.'

'So he was your uncle.' It was more a challenge than a question.

Jeff wasn't sure where this question-and-answer session was leading.

The front legs of the chair banged on to the board-walk as the man changed his position to a more upright one. Jeff tensed, sensing trouble.

The man stood and took a step towards Jeff, whose right hand migrated nearer the handle of his six-gun. The man took off his hat and extended a hand while offering a toothless smile.

'Bob Douthwaite. Pleased to make your acquaintance.'

He was younger than he looked despite the bald head. Jeff took the rough hand.

'Pleased to meet you, Mr Douthwaite.'

In the alley running alongside the store, a rough-sawn side door in the adjacent building opened with a loud squeak. Out came a cowboy adjusting his belt. His face wore the broadest of smiles. He nodded to Jeff and Bob as he passed by.

'Bob.' A woman's head appeared around the edge of the door. 'You're next.'

Bob Douthwaite looked a mite embarrassed. Cheeks flushed, he fidgeted with the brim of his hat. 'Well, Sheriff, nice talkin' with you. Gotta run. I'll stop by your office after my business here.'

'See you later,' Jeff called out.

The man shrugged his shoulders and hurried off down the alley. Jeff watched him go, not certain how he felt about his encounter with Bob Douthwaite. He shook his head. Whatever it was, he would find out in an hour or so. He looked up at the sky as it began to rain.

Not the heavy stuff, but a fine rain that coated everything with a multitude of tiny spots of water that seemed to soak into your skin.

5

Burke's Crossing, Yellowstone River, Montana

In the small bar-room at Burke's Crossing four men lounged at a table drinking rotgut whiskey.

'Let's get going.' The high-pitched voice belonged to a young cowboy dressed all in black. He stood tall and skinny, broad silver buckles gleamed on the crossed cartridge-belts and on the belt holding up his black pants. His name was Roy Cole, and he was mighty anxious to get to White Bluff.

Unhurriedly Ethan Todd leaned back in his chair and put his good foot on the stove at the side of the table. He took out the makings and proceeded to roll a cigarette, which he fabricated with great skill. He struck a match; the flame ignited first time and the end of the cigarette glowed as the flame took hold. He blew out a perfect ring of smoke with manifest enjoyment, as if it were to be his last. Todd smoked the stogie to its nub end, then stubbed the cigarette in an ashtray made out of bone. He rubbed his leg, grimacing with pain.

'Don't push me, kid,' he threatened.

A short stocky cowboy spoke. 'Let's not fall out over nuthin'.' Whitey Bell's words echoed around the bar.

Todd's voice softened, 'Don't let me down.'

'I won't,' said Whitey.

6

Double-J ranch

'What are you doing?' Jeff's voice was full of surprise. He'd seen the buckboard outside the ranch house.

Ika turned slowly; there were tears streaming down her cheeks. 'There's nothing here for me now my husband is dead.'

'But this is your home,' Jeff told Jim's widow.

'No, Jeff. Not any more. Our place is with my people.' She dabbed her eyes with a finely embroidered handkerchief. 'Jason feels he's more Crow than white. He has embraced the ways of my people.'

'But Sarah? She's . . .'

Ika lifted a finger to Jeff's lips. 'Don't say it, Jeff. It might not come out right.'

'I didn't mean . . .'

Again Ika halted him in mid-sentence. 'I know it's hard for you to understand, but our decision is final. I pray for your understanding and support.'

Jeff's heart sank. He nodded resignedly.

Ika threw her arms around him, wanting to comfort him; the warmth of her slender body pressed against him in true affection.

In another time, thought Jeff, he could easily have fallen in love with this woman; sometimes he felt he had done so already. He was sure she felt the same about him despite nothing having ever been said. Nothing had ever passed between them, other than would be expected between nephew and aunt, albeit Ika was of a similar age to Jeff.

Ika was first to break the moment, drawing away slowly. She looked deep into Jeff's eyes, sorrow filled her own; on tiptoe she kissed him on the lips, he returned her kiss, finding it difficult to leave it at that.

'Don't make this harder than it is,'

she pleaded, tears welling again in her velvet-brown eyes.

Jeff recovered his composure. 'Your mind is made up?'

She brushed away a tear. 'The Double-J is yours and the boys' now,' she said. 'It's what Jim wanted.' Ika turned back to her task of emptying drawers, carefully folding each garment before placing it into the open valise on the bed.

A noise behind him caused Jeff to turn. His heart was full. Sarah took a step into the bedroom; he was thankful she hadn't come in a few moments earlier, she might not have understood.

Sarah let the bag she was carrying fall to the floor with a clump, then she rushed into Jeff's open arms, nestling her pretty face against his chest.

Jeff stroked Sarah's raven-black hair and turned back to Ika with tears in his eyes. 'Don't do this,' he pleaded.

Ika closed her eyes as though it would give her strength.

'We are returning to my people.' She

tried hard but couldn't stop herself letting out one huge sob. 'It is all arranged,' she managed to say, turning away from Jeff's disbelieving gaze. 'Nothing anyone can say or do will deflect us from our decision.'

Jeff could not find any words.

Ika forced a smile. 'But,' she said, 'we'll be back to visit as often as we can. You will be heartily sick of the sight of us.'

'Never,' he promised, holding out an arm.

Ika slipped inside his embrace, joining her daughter. 'Tell me you understand,' she said.

'I'll try,' he answered.

'Big kiss,' Ika said, kissing Sarah's forehead, and Jeff on the cheek. 'Come on,' she said, drawing away. 'No sense prolonging the agony.' Ika led the way to the buckboard, Jeff toting their belongings.

He had just finished stowing away the luggage when Jason came out of the barn. He was leading three ponies.

'Look after these two,' Jeff told the boy, motioning to Ika and Sarah. 'They are very precious to me.' Jason nodded his understanding. Jeff grabbed the boy in a bear hug. 'You're special as well,' he said. Jason hugged him back.

The four of them stood silently for a moment, no one really wanting to break the bond. Tears flowed down all four faces.

Ika was first to get a grip on her emotions. 'Time to go,' she said resignedly, climbing on to the buckboard seat. Jason and Sarah climbed up next to their mother. Ika raised a hand. 'Bye.' She clicked her tongue and flicked the reins.

Jeff held on to Sarah's hand for as long as he could, until the speed of the buckboard forced him to let go. He watched the buckboard with the three ponies trotting behind, carrying away the three people that had an extra special place in his heart until they disappeared from view. None of them turned to look back.

Jeff was suddenly aware of someone crying. He turned. Standing on the ranch house porch Cheng Li was sobbing loudly, floods of tears soaked the front of his clothing. Jeff tried unsuccessfully to console the little Chinaman.

'Missie go! Missie go!' Cheng Li repeated tearfully. Jeff gave the Chinaman a comforting hug.

Jeff was racked with guilt as he rode back to White Bluff, not sure how he would feel if Laurie had any inkling of his feelings for Ika.

7

Burke's Crossing, Yellowstone River

'One down,' confirmed Ethan Todd.

Whitey Bell looked across at the big man. 'You really think this is a good idea, Ethan?'

'Nobody asked you to tag along,' growled Todd. His black eyes glowed with a fierceness that warned Whitey not to question their owner.

'I know, but I just wondered — '

'Don't wonder!' Todd snapped. 'Keep your nose out of my business.' He limped over to the window where Whitey was sitting.

For a split second Whitey was scared that Todd was going to hit him.

Todd looked out at the distant hills. 'Bastard Jacksons did this to me.' He pointed a finger towards his right leg. 'They're gonna pay for what they done.

Every minute of my pain they're gonna pay for.' He grimaced. 'Shall I cut *your* foot off an' a piece of *your* leg?' He leaned forward threateningly, drawing his hunting knife. He drew it across the air in front of Whitey's leg. 'And see how you like it?'

Whitey's eyes nearly popped from their sockets. Ever since he'd hooked up again with Ethan Todd he had seen signs of the wild madness that burned deep inside the big man. He recalled the day when Todd, then sheriff of White Bluff, had led a posse of gunmen to the Jackson ranch. Todd had been stomped by a horse. Busted his leg real bad. Gangrene had set in, ending up with the amputation of his foot and lower leg.

Whitey expelled a huge sigh of relief as he watched Todd put away the knife. He pondered for a moment. 'Why don't we just single each of 'em out. Kill 'em and get the hell out of here?'

Todd rounded on Whitey. 'No!' he yelled. 'Killin' 'em ain't gonna be that

easy. We gotta wait for the best chance.'
He calmed a little. 'Anyway, I'm takin'
my time. I want to savour every moment
of their pain for what they done.'

There was silence for a moment in
the crudely built cabin. Then Whitey
commented: 'We was lucky the other
day.'

'Luck never come into it.' Todd corrected. 'I staked out that calf on the ridge.
Baited 'im. Jim Jackson took the bait
and rode up to see what the problem
was, just like I planned.'

'Yeah, but it was lucky it was Jim that
rode up.'

'No! It was me! I planned it,' Todd
snarled.

Todd's jaundiced version was not the
one Whitey remembered. Another silence
descended. Whitey figured he was on a
loser trying to get Ethan Todd to accept
the huge degree of luck that had been
involved. He was getting mighty fed up
with Todd.

'Where's Cole?' Todd asked suddenly.

'Think he went into town,' Whitey replied sheepishly.

Ethan Todd's anger exploded. He kicked the door, almost losing his balance. 'I told 'im to stay round here. Don't want anyone to know we're here.' He paused a moment. 'I'm fixin' to ruin them Jackson boys. Kill 'em all. But they gotta suffer first. They'll be roundin' up their cattle soon. We'll be there to snatch the herd.'

'You sure them Luckett boys'll be with us?' Whitey asked.

'Sure. They won't let me down,' Todd growled.

8

The home of Sheriff Jeff Jackson and his wife Laurie, White Bluff

Jeff glanced out of the parlour window in the direction of the livery stable.

'Jeff.'

He turned to see Laurie walk in from the kitchen.

'Supper's nearly ready, if you want to wash up,' she said, placing a tray of crockery and cutlery on the table.

'OK,' he answered.

'Five minutes,' she told him. 'Will you get the twins to wash their hands? They're out back somewhere.' Laurie smiled.

Jeff took the towel she held out and went out to find Josh and Joel.

It didn't take him long to locate his two four-year-old sons. Their loud giggling gave away their position. He heard it as soon as he stepped into the back yard. Jeff wondered what new mischief they were getting up to.

The woodshed door creaked open, the air inside was dusty and chilly-cold. He pushed the door wider as a guilty silence descended. A shaft of daylight through the open door revealed the cause of the mirth. Josh stepped back abruptly, Joel was not as quick as his brother. Two pairs of sky-blue eyes set in two small faces looked sheepishly at their father.

On a slab of flat rock a large spread-eagled frog was still twitching, despite one of its hind legs having been severed. The still dripping bloody knife remained in the hand of the culprit.

Jeff held his temper. His humour was much more difficult to suppress: he wanted to laugh and ruffle their straw-blond hair.

'You had better put the poor animal out of its misery,' he told Joel.

The knife slipped from Joel's grip. Both boys stared blankly at their father, momentarily unsure how to react to the voice of authority.

'Cut its throat. Quick!' Jeff called out.

Josh picked up the knife, slicing through the frog's neck in one swift movement.

'Josh,' Jeff said loudly, 'bring the knife. Joel, get the spade and bury your victim out back. Then wash your hands. Both of you.' Then he added, 'Supper's ready. You had better hope it's not frog stew.'

Both boys made a face.

After the twins had gone to bed, Jeff and Laurie relaxed at the table over a cup of coffee. Laurie sliced a piece of apple cake and handed it to her husband. She had been horrified when Jeff had told her what the twins had done.

'I never thought they would be so mean.'

'Aw, they're just being boys.' Jeff nibbled the cake.

Laurie had still not come to terms with the fact that Jeff had not taken a switch to their backsides.

'Can't wallop them for every misdeed.' He drained his cup.

'I know. But I don't want them to grow up cruel,' she said sadly. 'Some of those older boys at school are a bit on the rough side. I'm certain that living here in town is not good for their development.'

Jeff knew where the conversation was heading.

'I can't resign, Laurie.'

'I know. It's just that I get so scared. Every time you leave the house I never know if you will be coming home.'

He placed a hand on hers. 'It's never been that bad.'

'You don't know what it's like, knowing your husband could be killed.'

'I think you're being melodramatic. It's not that dangerous.'

'I heard about the trouble with the Baston boys.' Laurie felt the need to support her argument.

'Well. Then you'll know that nothing happened. They'd had too much to drink. Ben and I locked 'em up for the night.'

'But you could have been killed.'

'No chance.' He smiled.

'Bobby Baston held a gun on you, didn't he?'

Jeff could see he wasn't going to win this argument. He finished the cake, and leaned back in his chair.

Laurie looked down into her lap, searching for the right words. 'Promise me you won't run for re-election?'

Jeff sighed in frustration. 'I've already told you I won't. Why won't you believe me?' He was irritated. Married life wasn't running smoothly at that moment. He shifted uncomfortably in his chair.

Laurie took Jeff's hand. 'I'm not sure I can cope with you being sheriff for another six months.'

He squeezed her hand. 'You still want to go East, don't you?'

She sighed deeply and nodded. 'I can't help it. I want the boys to have a better education than they will get here in White Bluff. I want them to have the best chance in life we can give them.'

Jeff pulled a face.

Laurie saw it. 'It's all right for you, Jeff, you love being sheriff. But it's not good for us.' She brushed away a tear. 'I don't want to lose you. I need you. The boys need a father. Couldn't Ben North take over?'

He dismissed her suggestion. 'He's not ready yet.'

She let go of his hand abruptly, a flush of colour rising to her cheeks. 'He never will be ready if it's left to you. Give him the chance. Let him show what he can do.' Laurie got up from her chair and went into the kitchen.

Jeff heard her sobbing. He walked to the window and glanced out absently at nothing in particular. There seemed no answer to the situation he found himself embroiled in, coming so soon after Jim's death, and Dan busting his leg. He tried hard to halt the direction his thoughts were moving in, but to no avail. How would Ika react in Laurie's situation? He recalled the sweetness of

Ika's kiss, her wonderfully cushioned lips. Not wanting to, but finding it impossible not to. What had happened to Laurie? She used to be a strong, fun-loving, self-reliant woman. Those were the qualities that had first attracted him to her. Had almost five years of marriage so dulled their passion that they were in danger of becoming merely companions? He fought shy of playing the 'what if' game, knowing it wouldn't lead to anything positive.

He needed time and space. He moved to the kitchen door, the sobbing grew louder. 'Laurie,' he called out, 'I'm going for a walk.' He didn't wait for an answer. 'Be back in a little while.' He closed the front door quietly.

★ ★ ★

Jeff stepped up on to the stoop outside the jail, having no recollection of walking there. He knocked four times. The clicking sound of a key turning the lock echoed into the night. Clay

57

Boothe's face peered round the door.

'Jeff!' he said surprised. 'What are you doin' here?'

Jeff tipped back his hat. 'Just needed a quiet spot for a while.'

'Trouble at home?' asked Clay.

'That obvious, eh?'

'Just a guess. Want some company or to be left alone?'

'I'll take a quiet half-hour. No offence?'

'None taken. Just brewed up a pot of coffee if you're interested.'

'Thanks.'

Clay poured out a cup of the steaming liquid and handed it over.

'Anyone in the cells?' Jeff enquired.

'No, it's been a quiet night.' Clay chuckled.

'Mind if I use one?'

'Heck no. You know where they are. Want a lantern?'

'No. Thanks.' Jeff opened the door to the cells and chose the first one. He set the cup on the floor, and fluffed up the pillow, then stretched out his long frame on the bed and closed his eyes.

The stark serenity of the cell was somehow comforting in a bleak kind of way.

Tonight wasn't his and Laurie's first fight, but of late the arguments seemed to come with greater regularity. Half the time he couldn't remember what the fights were about, but lately the subject of his resignation had more than dominated the subject matter. He knew how Laurie felt. He was sure he understood what troubled her, but did she understand how he felt? Probably not. She was right about one thing though — he did love being sheriff of Boulder County.

He reached down, his fingers groping for the cup. Just suppose he agreed to move back East, what would he do with his life? He was still a relatively young man. They had money. The cattle ranch was prospering, as was the wild mustang business. The silver mine was a bonus; the partnership with Ika's Crow Indian tribe was flourishing. All true, he reflected, but? And it was a huge BUT!

What would he do? He knew that living a life of leisure had no appeal for him. Socializing at tea parties with people he didn't know might be Laurie's dream, but it certainly wasn't his. Laurie had often spoken about how wonderful life in Boston would be, with Jeff working as a professor at the university.

He took a sip of the now tepid coffee. How often he had told her that teaching was not for him. In any case, dropping back into teaching would not be as simple as Laurie thought. No. Jeff Jackson needed excitement. Heck, that was why he, Clem and Dan had come to Montana in the first place. Dan's cousin, Billy Welch, had given his life for it.

'No!' he said out loud.

'What?' shouted Clay.

Jeff called back, 'Nothing. Sorry.'

Jeff shook his head. Living the idle life of a rich man was not for him. Laurie's words echoed around his head. 'We have to get the boys away from those McAlle brothers and that orphan kid, Walter Stiggert. All they want to do is play with guns and knives.'

'They're only four years old,' he remembered saying.

It was not that he didn't like it back East; he had taken Laurie back to Evansville two or three times to see his folks. And again, when the twins had been old enough to make the long journey. He had also taken her on a trip to Chicago. He remembered her saying how much she loved it. No dust. Civilized people. No guns. Fine clothes. Sophisticated food. She had said how remarkably cultured everything and everyone was.

Clay poked his head around the door. 'More coffee?'

'No thanks, Clay. I'd better be getting off home.' Jeff stood up.

'Everythin' sorted?' The young deputy asked.

Jeff shook his head. 'Not really, but it helped.' He opened the door to the street. 'Goodnight, Clay.'

' 'Night, Sheriff.'

9

A shack near Burke's Crossing

Ethan Todd took a long pull from the whiskey bottle. Killing Jim Jackson had been just great — the first of the breed. Being able to make it look like an accident had inserted a whole new dimension to Todd's plan: what if he could make every one of the Jacksons' deaths look like an accident? What a genius he was; the law would never look for him. Brilliant!

He had decided against killing Jim Jackson's squaw and kids; he didn't want to risk having Indians on his trail.

Roy Cole had not been happy with Todd's new plan, he liked the old uncomplicated plan much better. In that plan the Jacksons would die knowing who had killed them and why they had died. Roy wanted to face the men who had gunned down his brother — wanted to shoot each one of them. The inferno of vengeance burned deep in his soul.

'You're young,' Todd had told him, remembering the proverb he'd heard his father say many times: *Softly softly catchee monkey.* Well, he, Ethan Todd, had sure showed Roy how to 'catchee monkey' when he had bludgeoned Jim Jackson to death.

Todd cursed Roy's inability to do a good job. He was supposed to sneak into the Double-J and place burrs under the saddle blanket of any Jackson horse he saw. Todd cursed when he heard that Dan Jackson's fall had only resulted in a broken leg. Todd had hoped for a broken neck — still, Todd pondered, maybe gangrene would set in, and Dan would lose his leg just as he had. Maybe in the long run that would be better: more pain — a lifetime of pain. The more he thought about the notion, the more it appealed to him. Either way a busted leg would make

Dan Jackson easier to kill.

Todd exercised his mind with the conundrum of how to kill the remaining Jacksons. First off there was Clem Jackson: pushing him over a cliff? Drowning him in the river like an unwanted kitten? Lots of possibilities filled his head. He smiled to himself: any one of them would do. The death that would give him the most pleasure was Jeff Jackson's. He was their leader. How to kill him would need some powerful figurin'.

Each of the three men had his own reason for wanting to wreak havoc on the Jackson family. Each one's life had been made the poorer because of the Jacksons, following the disaster at the Double-J ranch five years earlier. Even Whitey Bell, normally an easy-going individual who followed the herd, hated the Jackson family. He had suffered many abuses in the penitentiary, often waking up from his nightmares screaming.

10

Double-J Ranch

Jeff turned to his wife. 'Laurie. I need to pick up some papers from the Double-J,' he said. 'Be back around supper time.'

Laurie watched her husband ride away, sensing an even greater change in him in the past few days. It was nothing she could put her finger on, not one specific thing or piece of behaviour, it was more than that. She shook her head and returned to the kitchen. Supper wasn't going to cook itself.

Five miles out from the Double-J Jeff met Cheng Li driving the buckboard into town, taking Dan to see Doctor Hollis. They would be staying overnight in town, Dan told Jeff. The Chinaman told Jeff that Clem and Sanchez and the rest of the hands were out on the range rounding up strays for branding.

'Place'll be deserted,' said Dan.

'No matter,' Jeff said. 'I'll get what I need. Maybe you and I can have a drink when I get back?'

'I'd like that,' said Dan.

Ika's pony was in the corral when Jeff got to the ranch, her saddle was set on the top cross-rail of the fence. Jeff's heart leaped. He unsaddled Atlas and ushered the big horse into the corral, then made his way across the yard to the sprawling ranch house with a spring in his step such as he hadn't felt for a long time.

Jeff pushed the open door wider. Ika had her back to him; she was sitting at the big oak desk, shuffling through papers.

The door creaked softly. Ika turned abruptly.

'Jeff!' She gasped, her brown eyes flashing their own greeting. 'I wasn't expecting to see you.' Her face flushed like a ripe strawberry.

He took off his hat, 'I needed a document for the bank.' His statement sounded like an apology.

She stood up. 'Me too. I left in a hurry the other day.' She looked down, suddenly remembering that moment.

'I'm glad you're here,' he told her, crossing the room. 'I didn't want to leave things the way we left them the other day.' He made to put his arm around her.

Ika held up a hand, stopping Jeff in his tracks. 'I believe in destiny, Jeff. You and I can't change it.' There was a deep sadness in Ika's eyes. 'Meeting your uncle Jim was my destiny. I was very young then, just a girl. He was tall, ruggedly handsome. We had fifteen happy years together. I wouldn't change one thing about my destiny.' She looked up into Jeff's face, tears welling in her almond-shaped eyes. 'I miss him so much.' She looked away, brushing away the tears that now rolled down her cheeks.

Jeff placed a hand over hers, squeezing gently, trying to tell her he understood.

Ika lifted her eyes to look again into his face: an honest face, she thought, straightforward, loyal, dependable, handsome. Jeff's features mirrored his uncle's in so many ways. Despite fighting her feelings, Ika couldn't help being drawn to him. She smiled a wan smile, her eyes saying *thank you*. Deep in her heart she held a great affection for Jeff.

'It's getting late,' she said. She rose from her chair, realizing the dangers to be found where her unbridled feelings wanted to take her, 'I should probably go.' Her words were unconvincing.

Jeff held on to Ika's hand, not wanting to break contact. They were close, he could hear her heavy breathing. His own heart pounded loudly in his chest, her breasts rose and fell with every breath. She was so beautiful. He couldn't help himself. He leaned forward as she raised her oval face towards his, kissing her softly on the lips, feeling her body move to his. His passion threatened to explode as his feelings for her surged through the whole of his body.

Ika responded, their bodies moving together in an instinctive embrace. Ika returned his kiss as both entwined their arms around each other. Each kiss and caress grew in intensity, climaxing when Ika drew away. She was breathless, her chest rising and falling heavily. Jeff's heart pounded, every fibre of his body aching for more.

'No,' Ika said softly. 'I have to go.' She pulled away from his reaching arms.

Jeff followed her to the door like an expectant puppy.

Tears rolled down Ika's cheeks as she turned. 'I love you, Jeff,' she said tenderly, 'but this will never work.'

Ika's statement stunned Jeff. To know she loved him as he loved her was something he had never thought possible, but to suffer such rejection only served to worsen his anguish.

She lifted up on to tiptoe and kissed him one last time, the palms of both hands pressed firmly against his broad chest. His eyes pleaded for more.

'We will never allow this to happen again,' she said abruptly. 'You go on home to Laurie and your children.'

Ika turned to leave.

'Ika!' Jeff called out.

She didn't turn back, but as she pulled the door open she said words Jeff hated to hear.

'We both know we must not let this happen.' Her abrupt words sounded so final. 'Come on, help me with my horse,' she said, disappearing through the door.

Jeff stood stock still, unable or unwilling to move, his heart still racing, pounding inside his chest like a thousand drummers.

It was true: he loved Laurie, but his passion was for Ika; he desperately wanted her. He needed to be with her, to join their bodies together. The sudden realization that this would never happen bore down on him like a lead weight.

The sound of movement outside pulled him out of his melancholy. She was leaving. He had to see her; he couldn't bear the thought of parting in this way.

He rushed through the door, almost stumbling head first off the porch. Ika had one foot in the stirrup. She glanced once over her shoulder, then gracefully threw her right leg over the pony's back.

Jeff looked longingly at one of the two women he loved. She sat astride her pony, tall and proud, regal and proud as the daughter of a chief should be: beautiful, but unavailable. His heart sank deeper, the aching in the pit of his stomach worse than any pain he had ever felt before.

She smiled a wan smile. Jeff wanted to remember her the way she looked at that moment. Ika held out a hand to him; he took it warmly, holding her slender fingers to his cheek. He kissed each in turn before she slowly withdrew them from his gentle grip.

'It will be hard for both of us, Jeff. Now more than ever. But in time we will come to accept that it is for the best. We both know that in our hearts.'

Jeff nodded his understanding, not really believing it.

Ika reached out a hand and touched his cheek. 'Goodbye,' she said softly. Her fingers stroked his skin, then she cantered away.

' 'Bye,' he called out loudly. 'My love,' he added in a whisper as she disappeared into the night.

Ika didn't look back.

Jeff slumped on to the porch steps and rubbed the tears from his eyes. Surely the ache in his heart would never stop. He suddenly felt sick, hating the situation he found himself in. He loved two women, both beautiful, but different in so many ways. One, blue-eyed, blonde and fair-skinned, the other dark-eyed, her olive skin coloured by the sun.

How long he sat alone watching the setting sun, he couldn't say. He wanted to cry again, but this time managed to force back the tears. Where were Clem and Dan when he so desperately needed them? Jeff needed a confidant, someone he could unburden his feelings to. Clem, his brother was the most likely candidate for the job, but he wasn't here — no one was here; the Double-J ranch was deserted.

Eventually he cried loud sobs of misery, until he could cry no more. In the house he washed the pain from his face, then saddled Atlas and rode to town — back to his wife and family.

11

The home of Jeff and Laurie Jackson, White Bluff

Laurie sat at her dressing-table as thoughts she wished she could push away whizzed around her head. Every one of her senses told her that something serious was troubling her husband. She kept going over and over what was troubling her, unable to focus on one thing. It wasn't just one thing, she told herself, it was a whole sequence of tiny changes.

She had always loved the way Jeff would sneak up behind her, particularly when she was standing at the bowl in the kitchen. He would wrap his strong arms around her, kiss her neck, breathe gently on her hairline, smooth his lips across the skin; it tickled so much she used to think she couldn't stand it. He would tell her how much he loved her. He hadn't done anything like that for several days. Come to think of it, he was much less attentive to her needs than at any time since their marriage.

He seemed all together much less tolerant of the children, too often shouting at them to be quiet when they were running around the house, as children do.

Her silent fear gripped her insides. Laurie wanted so much to ask her husband what was wrong, but she feared the truth. What if he had fallen out of love with her? What if the fault lay with her, not him? She examined her own behaviour minutely, recalling several instances when she wished she had remained silent. Could it really be her fault? Had she done or said something? A penny dropped loudly. She realized how many times she had brought up the subject of his resigning his position as Sheriff of Boulder County, but only because she worried about him so. But was it the truth that she worried more for herself and the boys than for him? No! she told herself. A resounding no! Perhaps she had mentioned this once too often. She so desperately wanted to up stakes and go to live back East. Was this the root cause of Jeff's unhappiness?

Absently Laurie picked up her hairbrush and ran the soft bristles through her long blonde hair, feeling and hearing the crackle of the tiny charges of electricity. She smiled ruefully — they had electric street-lighting back East.

She looked at the clock, surprised to see it was well after nine. Where was he, anyway? The twins had been tucked up in bed for some time. Jeff had promised to be back before supper time; that was over two hours ago. He had only gone to the Double-J to fetch some paperwork; how long should that take?

Laurie heard the heavy thud of the front door closing, followed by the sound of boots on carpeted floorboards. She tidied her hair and touched a spot of perfume behind her ears and between her breasts. She took a moment to put on her best lacy nightgown. A quick glance in the mirror told her she was ready. She picked up a lamp and went down to greet her husband.

He was in the kitchen, stripped to the waist, his broad back to her. She watched him rinse away the soap and begin to towel himself dry, loving the way his muscles bulged and rippled.

Jeff sensed her behind him. He turned and smiled. It was the smile of a troubled man, not of a man without a care in the world. He tugged his shirt from the back of a chair and pushed an arm inside one of the sleeves. Laurie set down the lamp and crossed to him. Without letting him get his other arm inside its sleeve she threw her arms around his neck and kissed him on the mouth as passionately as she could.

Jeff responded to her kiss, but not in the way Laurie had hoped. The depth of passion wasn't there as it used to be. It was as if Jeff was going through the motions: more tender than passionate. She hugged him to her, as though to prevent him from flying away.

He kissed the tip of her nose. 'Sorry I'm late,' he said. 'Took longer than I thought.'

'No worries,' she lied. 'Hungry?'

'Sure am.' It was Jeff's turn to lie.

The lump in Laurie's throat refused to budge. Hands still at the back of his neck, she bunched her fists, hoping the pain of her fingernails digging into her palms would help calm the turmoil in her breast.

'Good,' she said, calmer now. 'On the menu tonight,' she joked, 'we have beef stew. Or, if you prefer, I can fry you a big juicy steak.' Laurie relaxed her hands and ran her fingers through the small hairs on his neck.

'That tickles.' He laughed.

The sound of his laughter warmed her heart; it was what she wanted to hear. She couldn't remember the last time she had heard him laugh.

She stepped back half a pace, 'Well,

what's it to be, cowboy?' She giggled girlishly. 'Steak or stew?'

'Hmm?' He pondered. 'I think I'll take a plate of stew.' He smiled, allowing her to lead him by the hand to the dining table.

'Good choice.' She laughed. 'One plate of stew coming right up. Take a seat, sir.' She pulled out a chair and motioned for him to sit.

Laurie ran to the kitchen like a newly wed bride. She put the stew pan on the stove and put on her apron, suddenly happier than at any time in the past week.

In seconds she returned to his side, coffee pot in hand. 'Coffee?' she asked.

Jeff nodded.

Laurie poured out two cups, 'I'll take a cup with you,' she announced. 'Stew'll be just a few minutes.' Laurie sat down next to Jeff and placed one hand over his. 'Everything OK?' she purred.

Jeff was silent, brooding, staring away into space, as though searching for something. Once or twice he started to speak, but stopped before any words came out. He gave a slight shudder, then lifted her hand to his lips. He kissed it. Her skin tasted warm and slightly salty; he held it tightly. Laurie felt sure he was trying to find the right words before speaking, but he just kissed her hand again and stayed silent.

'What is it?' Laurie asked softly. A sob caught in her throat; she felt like crying but no tears came. She sat quietly, looking at her husband, wanting to say more.

Jeff pursed his lips and scrunched up his eyes. 'Nothing,' he said.

The way he spoke the word said a lot more to Laurie. That one word seemed to change the happy mood of the moment.

Jeff sighed deeply. 'Oh, I don't know.'

The lid on the metal stew pot clanked up and down. Laurie rushed to the kitchen.

Saved by the bell, thought Jeff.

He let his eyes wander through the open kitchen door to where Laurie was spooning his meal into a dish. She was lovely. Tonight she looked even lovelier in her lacy nightgown, the shapeliness of her long legs showed clearly through the fine material. Two children she had borne, and her figure was as perfect as the first time he had seen her. He loved her, of that there was no doubt, but his growing feelings for Ika had introduced many uncertainties.

Ika had captivated him the first time he had met her, but then she had been his uncle's wife and therefore unavailable. His infatuation for the vivacious Indian princess had grown the more he had got to know her. Jeff put his lustful feelings for Ika down to man's natural instinctual behaviour: men couldn't help where their brain was much of the time.

But Ika was free now. He knew it was wrong to fall for his dead uncle's wife, but what could he do about it? He felt powerless to control his feelings.

It was his fault. He constantly told himself that. He should have kept a respectable distance between Ika and himself. Regardless of his feelings for her, he should have continued to hold them inside and not allow them to burst out into the show of affection he had demonstrated when the two had met earlier at the Double-J. But at least Jeff now knew that Ika felt the same about him. It didn't help. It only served to make the pain of their parting more difficult to bear.

He knew he needed to get a grip. He was a married man. The sheriff of Boulder County. A pillar of local society. Folks looked up to him. How would the community react if they found out about him and Ika? He shrugged at the thought; what was there to find out, anyway? A couple of kisses and a quick fondle?

Laurie rested a hand on Jeff's shoulder as she set a bowl of stew in front of him. She trailed her fingers across the back of his neck as she walked around the table. She sat down opposite him. She had always loved watching him eat, he had always done so with such gusto.

Tonight was different. Jeff picked at his food, like a man with a full stomach being forced to eat more. It was almost as though he believed every mouthful to be poisonous.

Laurie sat in silence, wondering how to get her man to open up to her, to tell her what was troubling him.

Jeff pushed away the dish of half-eaten food.

'You didn't enjoy that,' Laurie said. It was a statement more than a question. 'Can I get you something else?'

Jeff shook his head. 'I'm not really hungry.'

She squeezed his hand. 'Want to talk about it?' She asked soothingly. His eyes held a surprised look. 'I can't fix it if you won't tell me what it is that's troubling you.'

Jeff looked away, avoiding eye contact. Not wanting Laurie to see the guilt that he felt was written plainly across his face.

Laurie's frustration threatened to boil over into anger. Theirs had always been an open kind of relationship. Now suddenly her man was distant, withdrawn. She couldn't stand it.

'Jeff!' she said, raising her voice a decibel or two. 'You have to tell me what is wrong.'

He gazed into her face, but said nothing, fearing she had guessed his guilty secret.

Laurie's patience was stretched to the limit; she squeezed his hand again. 'Tell me!' she snapped, almost shouting the order.

Her words seemed to snap Jeff out of his melancholy. 'I'm sorry,' he told her. 'I've been out to the ranch. Uncle Jim's death. He wasn't there. Brought it all home to me.' His words were delivered staccato style, in unconnected phrases, not coherent sentences. 'I'll be all right,' he said. 'Just give me a little more time.' He turned over his hand and squeezed hers.

Somehow Laurie knew he wouldn't be.

'I'm bushed.' Jeff yawned. 'Time for bed,' he said, rising from the table.

With a heavy heart Laurie extinguished all but one lamp. She raked the embers from the fire, sighing deeply, and followed her husband upstairs.

12

The sheriff's office, White Bluff

'Mike!' Jeff was surprised to see his old friend walk through his office door. Jeff's swivel-chair spun wildly as he leaped from behind his desk to greet Marshal Mike French. The two men shook hands warmly.

'How are you, Jeff?' Mike asked, clapping his friend on the shoulder.

'I'm well, thanks, very well. What brings you to White Bluff?'

'Got a couple of prisoners outside. Picked 'em up near Burke's Crossing.'

'Anybody I know?'

'Jack Kench and his brother, Bill.' Mike gestured towards the open door. 'You probably got papers on 'em. Need to borrow one of your cells for the night if that's OK?'

'Sure.' Jeff grabbed a bunch of keys from a hook on the wall.

'Need the services of your doc as well.' Mike looked a little sheepish. 'Bill took a slug in the arm. Local barber dug the slug out and slapped a bandage on him.'

Jeff's memory kicked in. 'Weren't the Kench brothers riding with the Luckett gang?'

'Yep. You got a good memory,' Mike commented. 'Asked 'em where the rest of the gang are, but they won't say nothin'.'

Outside the jail three riders sat their horses; two looked worse for wear.

'This young feller's Deputy US Marshal Steve Greenway,' Mike said, making the introduction. 'Steve. This is Sheriff Jeff Jackson. One of my best ever friends.'

Steve Greenway said hello.

'Bring them in,' said Jeff.

Mike drew his Colt and took a step towards the prisoners. 'All OK, Steve?' he asked the young deputy.

Steve Greenway nodded. To the prisoners he said, 'Look, boys, we found you a room for the night.' The two men gave the deputy a look of distaste. 'Step down careful like and don't try anything,' he ordered.

Jack Kench squinted against the harsh glare of the setting sun. 'Want to take these cuffs off, Marshal? Be easier,' he said with a grin.

'Easier for you, Jack. Not for us,' answered Steve. 'Come on, get going.'

Jack Kench shrugged, grabbed the saddle horn and swung a leg over his horse's back.

'Help your brother,' Mike ordered.

Jack helped his younger brother down from his horse, Bill's sleeve was heavily stained with dried blood. Jeff noticed there was dried blood on Jack Kench's collar.

Mike saw where Jeff's eyes were focused. 'Resisted arrest,' he said by way of explanation.

Spotting a boy running along the street, Jeff beckoned him over.

'Go tell Doctor Hollis I have a prisoner with a gunshot wound. Ask him if he can come take a look. Then go to my house. Tell my wife Mike French is in town. OK?' The boy waited, palm extended. Jeff smiled and gave the kid two bits. 'Seems like you have to pay everyone to do anything these days,' he said ruefully.

'Did you say Doc Hollis?' Mike asked.

'Yes.'

'Heck. I thought that old galoot would have been retired by now.' Mike smiled. 'Be good to see him.'

The cell door clanked shut behind the Kench brothers. Jeff turned the big key in the lock.

'Give me your hands,' Mike ordered.

Jack thrust his hands through the bars of the cell to allow Mike to remove the handcuffs. He helped his brother up, Mike took off Bill's cuffs.

'Needs a doc,' pleaded Jack.

'Relax,' Mike told him. 'The doc's on his way. Take it easy, this'll be your room for the night.'

'Any chance of sumpthin' to eat an' drink?' asked Jack.

'I'll get them some water,' said Jeff.

'Water!' Jack grimaced. 'We bin eatin' dust for hours. What about a whiskey to settle my stomach?'

'Shut up, Jack,' Mike shouted.

Jeff closed the cell-block door and locked it. Mike and his deputy took the seats Jeff offered. Jeff poured out three coffees.

Mike asked how everyone was. He was devastated when he heard the news of Jim Jackson's death.

'That man treated me like a son,' Mike said tearfully. He shook his head, 'Like a son,' he repeated.

Jeff ran through the circumstances.

'Don't seem possible. I can't believe he's dead,' Mike groaned.

'Neither can we,' said Jeff.

'How you holding up?'

'So so, I guess. Still haven't come to terms with it.'

The talk moved on to the state of the territory; the lawlessness along the frontier, politics, the situation in the territory's capital, Helena.

'Deputy governor confided to me that

he thought Montana wouldn't get state-hood for at least ten years,' Mike stated.

Steve took a second cup of coffee; Mike refused.

'Anyhow,' he said, 'how's the mustang business?'

Jeff couldn't hold back a smile. 'Army's still buying all we can catch. Beef's doing well too,' Jeff added, anticipating Mike's follow-up question.

'What about the silver mine?'

'Doing great.' Jeff grinned. 'Even sharing the profits with Ika's people it's a lucrative project.'

'I heard you was rich.' Mike laughed.

'Not rich,' Jeff corrected. 'Comfortable.'

'How's that lovely wife of yours?'

'Still lovely,' Jeff answered proudly. 'You and Steve will dine with us tonight, won't you?'

'Try and keep me away,' Mike replied eagerly.

'We have a spare bed, so you won't have to walk far afterwards.'

'I hope you and Laurie won't mind,

but I'd prefer to bed down here at the jail. I want to keep my eyes on these two.' He gestured towards the cells with a nod of his head.

'You expecting trouble?' asked Jeff.

'Not especially. But I'll feel happier if I'm here. Better safe than sorry. Steve will stay with me.'

'As I said, Steve's welcome to eat with us as well.'

The deputy shook his head. 'Thanks for the kind thought, Sheriff,' he said, 'but I'll stay here with the prisoners. Eat when they eat,' he said.

'I'll organize some supper for you. Big steak and fried potatoes be OK?'

'Bigger the better. Appreciate it,' answered the deputy. 'Steak for them?' he asked.

'Heck, no,' corrected Jeff. 'They'll get beef stew, and like it.' Jeff looked up at the clock. 'My deputy, Clay Boothe'll be here in ten minutes. He's got the graveyard shift.'

Heads turned as the door opened. It was Clay.

'Got Doc Hollis here with me,' he said. 'Tells me we got a wounded prisoner. Who got shot?' His question trailed away when he saw Jeff had company.

Doctor Horatio Hollis brushed past Jeff's young deputy. He saw Mike and let out a yell.

'Mike French!' He exclaimed. 'What a surprise. Good to see you, boy.'

The two men embraced.

'Hello, Doc.' Mike smiled, thrilled to see another old friend.

When Bill Kench's wound had been tended to and Doctor Hollis had left, Mike turned to Jeff.

'Say. Did you hear about our friend Ethan Todd?'

'Sheriff Todd?' asked Clay. 'Sorry. Ex-sheriff,' he corrected.

'That's the one,' Mike said, turning back to Jeff.

'No. Why what's happened?'

'He got out of the penitentiary some months ago. Seems he teamed up again with Whitey Bell and a coupla other ex-Brown's gunhands. Went into the hold-up business. Should get a flyer on him soon.'

'I hadn't heard,' said Jeff. 'Where's he been operating?'

'Wyoming way. Law nearly caught up with him a coupla times. Lots of people identified him; limps, foot amputated in prison. Wouldn't be surprised to hear he's back in Montana. He always swore he'd get even.'

Jeff dismissed the potential threat as unlikely.

On the walk to Jeff's house Mike said, 'I had another reason for coming to see you,' he confessed.

'I wondered why you'd make such a long detour.'

Mike held up his hands in mock surrender. 'Guilty as charged, Sheriff. Don't shoot,' he joked.

'OK. Tell me.'

'The governor's more concerned about the amount of lawlessness in the territory than you would imagine. Also, he's worried about the number of citizens' vigilante committees being formed. He's thinking of forming an elite corps of territory rangers. Similar to Texas.'

Jeff was surprised. Something certainly needed to be done.

'Good idea,' he opined, pausing to allow his friend to continue.

'Deputy governor wanted me to sound you out.'

'As I say, I think it's a good idea.'

Mike gritted his teeth. 'There's more to it than that. He wants you to head up a unit.'

'What? Move to Helena?'

'No. He and the governor favour setting up four separate groups. You'd head up the south-eastern corps. The other corps would be in Helena, Virginia City, and Fort Benton. Any thoughts?'

'It's not a bad notion, but the devil will be in the detail.'

'All the governor wants to know at this stage is if he can count on your support.' Mike reached over to his coat and dug out a sealed envelope from the inside pocket. 'This letter'll explain everything.'

Jeff stopped under one of the town's streetlights. He slit the seal and read the contents twice over. He contemplated for a minute or two, examining the initial pros and cons that came into his mind.

Mike saw Jeff's hesitation, mistaking it for negativity. 'Don't give me your answer now,' he said. 'Think about it tonight.'

Jeff nodded. 'OK, but no mention of this in front of Laurie.'

Mike sensed a threat of female hostility to the idea. 'Cross my heart,' he promised.

13

Burke's Crossing, Yellowstone River

Eli Luckett cursed loudly. 'You sure?' he yelled.

'Pos'tive,' replied Amos Burke, wiping a glass with a cloth that was none too clean.

Eli spat on the sawdust covered floor of the dingy bar. 'When?'

'Yes'dy.' Amos told him. 'Jack was leanin' on the bar, me an' him was havin' a jaw.' He spat on the cloth, 'Bill was sittin' at that table.' He nodded his head towards the specific piece of furniture, then continued with his story. 'In come the marshal. His deputy was totin' a shotgun.' He sniffed as if this had impressed him. 'Marshal said, 'Jack Kench you're under arrest, you too Billy'.

'He told 'em to loosen their gunbelts, stand up, and step away. Jack did as he

97

was told. Billy went for his gun. God dang it!' He let out a whistle. 'That marshal had the fastest draw I ever did see. Shot Billy's gun clear out of his hand afore he'd even got his piece up and cocked. The deputy smashed a shotgun into the side of Jack's head. He was out for a while, but come to later.'

'Marshal was fast, you say?'

'Light'nin'.'

'Faster'n me?'

'I never said that, Eli.'

Eli sneered. 'Billy Kench was never very fast,' he said. 'Where'd they take 'em?'

'T'the jail in White Bluff. Heerd the marshal say so meself,' Amos boasted.

'Gimme a whiskey,' Luckett ordered. 'Clean glass,' he added. 'Give 'em all whiskey.'

Eli tossed a few coins on to the bar. The six remaining members of the Luckett gang stepped forward eagerly.

'Curly.'

A big man with a white scar across one cheek grunted in response to Eli's call. 'You know White Bluff.' Luckett didn't wait for any sign of confirmation. 'What's the law like there?'

Curly thought for a moment. 'Sheriff, plus a coupla deputies.'

'Gunslingers?'

'Nope. Just regular peace officers.'

Eli turned back to Amos Burke. 'Just a marshal an' one deputy, you said?'

'Far as I know.'

'OK. We'll go into town tonight and break 'em out. I need 'em for the job I got in mind.'

White Bluff

'Keep that hoss quiet,' whispered Eli Luckett.

The seven desperadoes had walked their horses, plus two spares, around the back of White Bluff's buildings.

'Loose-hitch 'em,' Luckett ordered, looping the reins of his horse over a fence cross-rail. His men followed his lead. He turned. 'You two go down that alley there at the side of the jail.' He pointed. 'You two make your way round that way, wait for my signal. Curly, you an' Ace follow me.'

Bold as brass Eli Luckett marched up to the door of the sheriff's office, his two cohorts close behind. Inside, the blinds were down but lights burned brightly. Luckett looked round once, then turned the doorknob — the door wasn't locked. Six-gun in hand he pushed the door open and stepped into the doorway. His eyes darted around the office, taking in every corner. Several lanterns were lit but the office was deserted.

'Hello!' he called out. No one answered. 'This is gon'be easier'n I figured,' he said under his breath. He stepped to one side. 'Ace. Inside. Find the keys,' he ordered. 'Desk first,' he added as Ace Gogerty squeezed past.

'Hold it!' a loud voice commanded.

Instinctively Eli Luckett took a half-step backwards. Inside the office Ace Gogerty went for his gun.

The deafening blast of a shotgun boomed through the confined space, Ace cried out in pain as a hail of buckshot tore into his flesh.

'Take cover,' Luckett called out, backing away further.

'Luckett! Eli Luckett!'

Luckett spun round in the direction of the shout.

'Federal officers. Throw down your weapons,' Mike French ordered.

Luckett's turn brought him face to face with two peace officers standing in the middle of the street. Reflected lamplight sparkled from the badges pinned to their chests.

In the alley his two men lay unconscious; Deputy Ben North was watching over them. Two others lay in the street; neither was moving.

Eli Luckett knew he was in a bad place, silhouetted against the lights of the sheriff's office. His Colt was still in his hand, but he had allowed his arm to fall to his side. It was a tight spot, but he had been in many tight spots before.

He knew he was fast with a gun. And he was fearless. When some men froze, he didn't.

A quick glance sideways told him he was alone. Curly had edged away along the stoop, arms raised high above his head.

Eli Luckett raised his six-gun. Marshal Mike French was faster. Eli's spent bullet kicked up the earth midway between the two groups of men. Mike's bullet slammed into Eli's chest, propelling his body backwards, arms flailing, legs kicking, until he hit the timber wall of the office with a thud. Eli fell forward, firing one more shot; the bullet smashed harmlessly into the boardwalk. His bent right leg shook once, then straightened out and was still.

Curly Maddern, the only member of the Luckett gang still standing, feared the worst. He stood like a statue, hearing the mechanical sound of shells clicking into place, feeling a wetness spread through the patch of trouser material between his legs. He shoved his hands even further above his head, well clear of his pair of six-guns.

'Don't shoot, Marshal,' he yelled.

'Drop your gunbelt,' Mike ordered. 'One hand.' The outlaw did as Mike ordered,

'Step away,' Mike told him. 'Gather 'em up, Steve.' Mike turned to Jeff, who like him was holstering his six-gun, looking around at the bodies. Mike said, 'You'll need a bigger jailhouse if this continues.' He laughed. A few of the gang were recovering consciousness. Steve Greenway collected their guns.

Deputy Ben North prodded his shotgun into the backs of the Luckett gang. Then, with the help of Clay Boothe and Steve Greenway, he herded them to the jail.

'We're gonna need some help getting this bunch back to Helena. Can you lend me one of your deputies?' asked Mike.

'Don't see why not,' answered Jeff.

'Gonna leave you a bit short-handed?'

'Don't worry about it. We got a

couple of special constables who help us out from time to time. Also, Clem and Dan won't mind taking a turn.' Jeff suddenly saw an opportunity to get away from White Bluff for a time. 'I might come with you,' he said.

'Be mighty pleased to have you,' Mike replied.

14

Burke's Crossing, Yellowstone River

Refreshed from his long nap, Ethan Todd pulled on his boots. The leather was well worn, he noticed; he would soon need new ones. The crazy thing was that it was the right boot that pinched his foot something awful, despite that foot being made of wood. He stamped into them then hitched up his gunbelt. He grabbed his coat, then hobbled out to his horse.

The short ride to Amos Burke's took only a few minutes. The lights in the bar shone bright against the night sky. Todd hitched his horse to the rail outside and went inside.

'Ethan,' greeted the barkeep.

'Amos,' Todd replied, taking out the makings. He rolled a thin cigarette and looked round for a match. 'Say,' he asked, 'did I hear horses a while back?'

'Sure did.' Todd looked quizzically at the barkeep. The big man caught on, 'Eli Luckett and his gang.'

'Luckett?' Todd queried.

Amos grinned. 'Yep. Rode to White Bluff. Said sumpthin' 'bout the Kench brothers.'

Todd grunted. 'What about 'em?'

Amos shrugged. 'Didn't I say?'

'No, you never said nuthin' 'bout the Kenches.'

'Sorry, Ethan.'

Amos Burke repeated what he had earlier told Eli Luckett.

Todd slapped the bar with the flat of his hand. 'Why didn't you tell me this before?' he demanded.

'Never thought. Sorry. Was it important?'

A horse pulled up outside. Boots sounded on boards. The door swung open. In rushed Whitey Bell. He was obviously in a hurry, his face was paler than if he'd seen a ghost.

'What's up?' Todd asked.

Whitey ignored the question. 'Gimme a whiskey, quick,' he called to Amos. His voice was all shaky.

Burke poured out a tot. Whitey grabbed the glass and gulped down the fiery liquid. 'Another,' he gasped.

Todd pushed Whitey's shoulder. 'I asked you what's up?' he repeated irritatedly.

Whitey was still out of breath. 'Shot or taken,' he said, grabbing the bottle from Burke's hand, raising it to his lips.

'Who's bin shot?' Todd shouted.

Whitey paused his gulping only to say one word. 'Luckett.'

Todd snatched the bottle out of Whitey's grip. 'Luckett shot? Tell me what happened?'

Whitey tottered backwards, feeling for a chair. He found one and sat down heavily, fighting to get his breath.

'Well?' shouted Todd.

Whitey took a deep breath. 'Mike French shot Eli. In town. Outside the jailhouse. Ace Gogerty's dead. Rest of the gang's locked up tight.'

'Is Eli dead?'

'Stiff as a plank,' Whitey answered. 'The two Kench boys are locked up as well.'

'What about Curly?'

'In jail.'

Todd swore more profanely than usual. He took several long gulps from the bottle he'd snatched from Whitey, then threw the empty bottle into the fireplace.

He turned back to Whitey and grabbed the cowboy by his coat collar. 'Where's Cole?'

Whitey shrugged his collar from Todd's grasp. 'Ain't seen 'im.'

Ethan Todd slumped on to a chair next to Whitey. He was lost for words. Whitey's news had scuppered his plans. His mouth opened and closed repeatedly but other than the occasional profanity no words came out.

Whitey looked at Todd, then found the courage to speak up. 'Ethan, I'm pullin' out in the mornin'.'

Todd glanced at the cowboy with hate-filled eyes.

Whitey averted his eyes. 'I ain't got the stomach for any more of this, Ethan.

Life's too short,' he said shakily. 'I'm headin' West.'

Todd's dark eyes narrowed. 'You,' he poked his index finger into Whitey's chest, 'ain't goin' nowhere. Hear me? Nowhere, till we finish what we came here to do.'

Whitey looked down at his trembling hands; his stomach churned with fear. He wished he could take back what he had said about pulling out. He should have kept quiet. Just gone.

'You hear me?' Todd yelled in his ear. 'Nowhere,' he repeated, his anger erupting like a volcano.

'I got to, Ethan.' Whitey trembled. 'You gotta understand.'

Todd rose slowly, kicking backwards with his left heel. The chair clattered against the far wall of the bar room.

'Stand up,' he said coldly. Whitey didn't move. 'I said stand up, you yella-livered skunk.'

'No, Ethan. No!' Whitey stammered.

Todd shoved the table sideways. 'Draw,' he said. The menace in his voice told

Amos Burke not to interfere.

'No, Ethan,' Whitey whimpered.

'Draw, I said.'

Knowing he couldn't outdraw Todd, Whitey made the mistake of allowing his right hand to twitch. To Ethan Todd, looking for an excuse to shoot the cowering man before him, the slight movement was enough to convince him that Whitey was going for his gun.

Whitey's anguished expression stayed in place as he crashed backwards with a bullet from Todd's Colt buried deep in his stomach.

Crimson blood gushed from the cowboy's open but speechless mouth, gurgling in his throat as he gasped for air, his eyes filled with pain and disbelief.

Ethan Todd stood over the twitching body, watching the blood pump from the wound, the front of the cowboy's grey flannel shirt now completely dark-red wet. Whitey tried to say something, but couldn't; then he lay still, eyes staring blankly at the ceiling.

Todd suddenly realized what he had

done. The enormity of his actions hit him hard: killing an ally was never a good thing to do.

Roy Cole walked in, looked at the supine body of Whitey Bell, then at Todd. The Colt in Todd's hand was still smoking. Cole instantly knew what had happened.

Todd glanced in his direction. 'He said he was pullin' out,' was all he said. He stood stock still for a few moments before holstering his gun. He found a chair and sat down.

Behind the bar Amos Burke stood like a statue; he was determined to stay silent.

The door banged shut. From outside came the sound of galloping hoofs, loud, but fading as horse and rider put distance between himself and the bar.

Todd looked around as though coming out of a trance. 'Where's Cole?'

'Gone,' Burke replied. His hand was resting on the stock of the double-barrelled shotgun he kept loaded behind the bar.

Todd was quiet for several minutes,

thinking through the events of the past few moments. Whitey dead, Luckett too. Cole gone. The rest of the Luckett gang in jail. The game was up. It hurt Todd to admit that his planned orgy of vengeance would never happen. The pain in his leg and foot was unbearable; it seemed to be getting worse, not better. He drew his Colt, cocked it, and set it down on the table.

Unsure of what Todd planned, Burke had the shotgun up and levelled — he wasn't about to take any chances.

Todd shook his head wildly from side to side, the full realization of the night's events heavy on his conscience. He brushed away the negative thoughts; now all he could think of was flight. Only one more thing needed to be done. Never leave a witness — it was a phrase he'd lived by all his life.

Slowly his hand closed around the grip of his Colt. Todd snatched up the weapon and turned to fire. He only got halfway before the buckshot from both barrels of Burke's shotgun blew away half his face. Todd's blood and brains decorated one wall of the bar room; his lifeless body slumped to the floor, shook violently for a second or two, then was still. Amos Burke threw up.

Half an hour later Burke locked the door and saddled his horse. He rode sombrely to town to report what had happened. He still felt sick; he had never before killed a man.

Free at last from fear, Amos Burke was able to tell all he knew about the death of Jim Jackson. One night he had overheard Ethan Todd brag to Whitey Bell about how he had killed the rancher.

★　★　★

Jeff re-read the Governor's letter for the tenth time. Laurie had seen the seal and had recognized that the letter was important. She fussed around her husband, waiting to see what the thick envelope contained, hardly able to contain her excitement.

Jeff would have had to be blind not to see his wife's impatience. He decided he needed to say something.

'Appears Montana's bucking for statehood.' He looked up. 'Apparently I am one of twenty Montana citizens invited to attend a conference in Helena.'

'The Territory capital?' Laurie screamed with delight. 'When do we leave?'

'Sorry, darling. Only me that's been invited.'

Laurie was crestfallen.

'I'll be leaving later this morning,' he announced, 'I'll help Mike deliver the prisoners. Kill two birds with one stone.'

Laurie fought back a tear. 'When will you be back?'

'Shouldn't take more than a week. I'll telegraph when I know what's intended.'

15

White Bluff

Laurie Jackson shivered. 'Is this cold spell ever going to end?'

'What's that?' her father asked.

'I said, it's cold.' She sniffed to add emphasis.

Lars Andersen shoved a bolt of cloth on to a shelf. 'When you expect Jeff to get back?'

'Day after tomorrow, providing the stage line don't decide to suspend the service again.' She grabbed her shawl from the back of a chair and threw it around her shoulders. 'Jeff wired the day before yesterday to say he was leaving Helena.' She pulled the shawl tight.

Both turned sharply to face the crashing sound that came from the stockroom.

'If your two monsters have broken something I'll . . . ' Lars let the threat trail away as he rushed to the door.

At fifty-four Lars Andersen was still sprightly. His hawklike eyes seemed to see everything. He rose most mornings at five, and by 6.30 had the doors of his general store open for business.

Laurie followed close on her father's heels.

The stockroom door creaked open before Lars reached the handle. Father and daughter heard a couple of muffled titters. Josh's tousled head popped around the door.

'Sorry, Grandpa. It was an accident.'

Laurie was first to react. 'Get out here. You too, Joel.'

The door opened slowly; the twins emerged even more slowly, Josh first, followed by his brother. Both looked guilty as hell but, like most children, both were stifling giggles.

In one hand Josh held the broken base of a glass storage jar, in the other he held the top. Both had jagged edges.

Laurie fought to maintain an even-tempered reaction. 'Give that to me.'

Josh handed over the broken jar.

Lars spoke up. 'No harm done,' he said. 'But,' he added, 'I'll take the cost out of your pocket money.'

Disappointment showed clear on the boys' faces.

'What was in the jar?' Laurie demanded.

Josh looked at Joel, then back to his mother. 'Candy,' he admitted sheepishly.

'Where is it?' Laurie was still fighting to keep her anger from erupting.

Josh looked down, playing with his entwined fingers. Joel stayed behind his brother.

'Answer me!' Laurie shouted.

'On the floor,' Josh mumbled.

'What?'

'On the floor,' Josh said louder as the doorbell tinkled brightly, heralding the entry of Clem Jackson.

'Lars. Laurie. Boys,' he greeted. 'What's going on?' he asked, puzzled by the various expressions facing him.

'Nothing much,' answered Lars with

a chuckle, running a hand through Josh's mop of hair. 'Just these two imps trying to break everything in my store.'

'Wrecked it, have they?'

'No!' chorused the boys.

'A broken candy jar, that's all,' Lars said.

Clem looked from the boys to Laurie. 'Any coffee going,' he asked, trying to take the sting out of the situation.

Laurie relaxed, and with this the tension in the room eased considerably. 'I'll get you a cup,' she said.

'Boys,' Lars said, 'let's go clear up the mess.' He beckoned, 'Then you can help me in the stockroom.'

Josh and Joel looked at their mother. Laurie nodded. The boys exchanged relieved grins and followed their grandfather.

'You buying?' Laurie asked, leading her brother-in-law to the tiny kitchen.

'No. Delivering.'

Laurie looked puzzled.

'Message from Jeff. Came in whilst I was in the telegraph office. He expects to get in tonight.'

'Tonight?' Laurie's surprise showed. 'You sure?'

Clem held out the telegram. 'Says so, don't it?'

Laurie read the message a second time and smiled, her heart warming to the notion that her husband would be with her sooner than anticipated.

'Last stage gets in around five, doesn't it?' she enquired.

'Yep, around five,' agreed Clem. 'Should be here for supper.'

16

White Bluff

Shielding his eyes from the low evening sun Sheriff Jeff Jackson stepped down from the stagecoach, brushing the dust from his coat. He stretched and stamped the circulation back into his cramped legs and feet. He turned his attention to the shotgun guard, who tossed his carpet-bag down.

Jeff caught it. 'Thanks Joe,' he said.

The stage-line clerk untied Jeff's horse from the back of the stagecoach. 'Want me to have your horse put in the livery stable, Sheriff?' he asked, looping his braces over his shoulders.

'Yes,' replied Jeff, 'that would be good of you.' The guard handed down Jeff's saddle to the clerk, and Jeff accepted the Winchester the clerk held out to him.

'Jeff!' shouted Clem.

Jeff swivelled at the familiar sound of his brother's voice.

'Good trip?' enquired Clem, taking the carpetbag and rifle from his elder brother.

'Dusty,' Jeff answered.

There came a shout of 'Sheriff!'

Jeff and Clem turned round.

'Good to see you, Ben.' Jeff held out his hand to greet his number one deputy. 'Anything happening?'

'Nope. Town's all quiet,' Ben North answered, 'and before you ask, no, we don't need you to come on duty.' He smiled, 'You get on home, see that lovely wife of yours, and the kids. Me and Clay'll keep a lid on everything.'

Jeff held up his hands in mock surrender. 'OK,' he said, 'I can take a hint. See you first thing in the morning.'

'No. You have a lie-in and a leisurely breakfast. Come in after lunch,' the deputy suggested.

'OK.' Jeff grinned. 'And Ben' — the deputy looked back — 'thanks. I appreciate it.'

Clem called out goodnight as Ben walked away. 'I'll walk you home, Laurie's expecting you.'

17

White Bluff

At 8.15 a.m. the three Paulson brothers, Webb, Abe and Zeke, and two of their henchmen sat their tired mounts on a ridge above the town of White Bluff.

'You're sure the sheriff's out of town?' Abe Paulson drawled.

'Certain sure,' answered Zeke. 'Won't be back till next week.' Abe's brother grinned a toothless grin. 'Only two deputies to worry about.' Zeke picked something out of his ear. 'How much you reckon we'll get?'

'We'll see,' snapped Webb, 'but should be a good amount.'

Jack Stowe, the sixth member of the Paulson gang, reined in his horse amid a cloud of dust.

Saddle leather creaked as Webb Paulson turned. 'Jack.'

Jack touched the brim of his hat.

Webb looked at his two younger siblings and the others. 'Bob. You and Tex skirt the town and come in from the south. The rest of us'll come in from the north. Meet in the alley behind the saloon. Jack, you'll take care of the horses. At five minutes after nine we hit the bank. OK?'

All five nodded or grunted out a 'yes'.

'Me'n Abe'll look after the manager. Bob and Tex'll watch any customers who're there. Zeke'll get the money from the cashiers. Whole thing should only take ten minutes. Any questions?'

None came. 'Anyone gets in the way, shoot 'em.' He looked at Jack, a mean-looking *hombre* with part of one ear missing.

Jack nodded. 'Fresh mounts are in the canyon we rode through yesterday. Good saddle ponies, got 'em locally.' He laughed.

★ ★ ★

Deputy Clay Boothe looked up from cleaning his Winchester as the door swung open. 'Mornin', Ben. Sleep well?'

'Not really,' Ben answered. 'Couldn't get to sleep. Sumpthin's eating at me and I can't figure what it is.' He added, 'Coffee on?'

'Yep. Fresh brewed.'

'What's the weather like now?' Clay asked.

'Sun's burned off that dirty-grey mist. Might see some drizzle. Maybe not,' Ben replied, shaking some dregs out another cup and filling it with steaming liquid.

Clay held out another cup. 'Pour me one too, will you?'

Ben looked at the big wall clock behind the sheriff's desk. 'Half past eight. We'll take a turn around the town.'

Clay looked at the deputy. 'After the coffee?'

Ben nodded. 'After the coffee.' He grinned. 'Finish cleaning your Winchester.'

'OK, nearly finished.' Clay saw Ben look at the other weapons on the rack,

'I got an early start. Cleaned and oiled all the rifles and shotguns.'

Ben smiled at his protégé. 'Good man.'

In the six months since Jeff had taken on Clay Boothe the young man had proved to be popular and able. Clay had drifted into town one day looking for work, his dishevelled appearance out of kilter with his youthful good looks. At that time, Clay had been a real-life waif and stray. Now, he was a smartly turned-out officer of the law. At twenty-two years of age he was three years Ben's junior.

Ben North was an experienced lawman, having started his working life as a farmhand, moving on after six months to a job as a trail-hand. Then, like Clay, he had been befriended by the sheriff of a town in Idaho who had taken him on as a part-time deputy. Three years ago Ben had applied successfully for the vacant deputy job at White Bluff. Jeff Jackson saw Ben as his natural successor.

'Jeff coming in today?' asked Clay.

'I told him to stay home till after lunch.' Ben drained the last of his coffee. 'Ready?'

'Yep,' Clay answered, standing up.

Ben moved to the gun rack, lifted down a double-barrelled shotgun, snapped it open and shoved in two cartridges; the shotgun closed with a *pop*.

Clay loaded the Winchester and operated the lever, pleased to hear the mechanical click of a shell easing into the chamber.

Ben turned the handle and opened the door. 'Nice morning,' he said, pulling down the brim of his Stetson to shield his eyes, 'Town looks quiet. Let's hope it stays that way.' He grinned.

* * *

Laurie was sitting beside the fire when Jeff came downstairs.

'Morning, Laurie. Been up long?' he asked.

Laurie looked up from her sewing,

127

and smiled. 'About an hour.'

Jeff leaned over and kissed his wife.

'Sarah and Jason are coming over later,' she told her husband.

'Ika?' he asked, then worried that he'd responded too quickly.

'I'm still hoping Ika will come with them, but somehow I don't think she will.' Laurie set down her sewing on a small table, her cheeks glowing, 'Hungry?'

'Sure am.' He grinned.

'Eggs and bacon?'

'You sure know the way to a man's heart.' He gave her another kiss, followed by a hug and a twirl around the parlour.

'Get off, you big galoot.' She giggled girlishly, planting a big kiss on his lips. 'Coffee and biscuits are on the table.'

This was the old Jeff; Laurie revelled in the change in him since his return. The man she loved was back. Last night had been wonderful; they had made love for the first time in an age. She felt like a newly-wed.

Fully replete, Jeff wiped his chin with

a napkin, then rubbed his belly. 'That hit the spot,' he called out to Laurie in the kitchen.

'Glad you enjoyed it,' she called back.

Jeff stretched and yawned, then got up and crossed the room to the hat-stand. Laurie entered as he was strapping on his gunbelt. He saw his wife's expression.

'What's the matter, honey?'

'I hate it when you put that on, you know I do.' Then she bit her lip, wishing she hadn't said anything.

He tied down the holster to his leg, then moved to where she was standing. 'It's part of my job, Laurie, you know that.'

Her eyes took on even more sadness. Words she had been determined not to utter issued uncontrolled from her lips. 'I don't want you to stand for re-election,' she said.

Her sentiment didn't surprise Jeff; they had spoken about the subject many times. He knew how she felt but the timing of her comment did surprise him; the elections were still several months away.

He put an arm out. 'Come here,' he said.

Laurie stepped into his embrace.

'OK,' Jeff said ruefully, 'when my current term ends we'll go back to ranching. I promise.'

Laurie kissed her husband. 'I'll hold you to that,' she said.

★　★　★

The air had a chill to it that tickled a person's nose hairs. The two deputies began the morning round of the town, chatting away happily, teasing each other with comments.

The town of White Bluff was laid out in the form of the letter 'T'. Main Street formed the stem of the 'T' with North Street and South Street running out on either side.

Near the livery stable a half-whispered voice was heard.

'Ben.'

The deputy swung round, it was the old hostler.

'I just seen a suspicious-lookin' dude ride round back. Thought you'd want to know.'

'When exactly?' queried Ben.

'About ten minutes ago. Thought it was odd he wasn't ridin' down Main Street.'

'What'd he look like?'

The oldster thought for a moment. 'Black ten-gallon hat, droopy moustache, guns everywhere.'

'Thanks, old-timer,' Ben said. 'Clay, you go along Main Street. I'll go down the alley and work my way along to the back of the livery. We'll meet up at the saloon. One whistle if you see anythin' suspicious.'

'Right,' Clay answered.

'Clay.' The young deputy turned. 'No heroics, OK?' Ben cautioned.

'OK'

Dust swirled in the wind as White Bluff slowly began to come alive. Clay strode carefully but purposefully along the boardwalk, his boots clumping solidly on the wooden boards. His stomach tingled with excitement. What old Jasper had seen probably wouldn't amount to anything, but it needed checking out.

Ben hugged the livery stable wall as long as he could, then moved cautiously to the corral fence. The lone rider Jasper had described was nowhere to be seen. The town clock ticked towards nine.

'Anything?' Ben asked Clay when they met up.

'Not a thing. Did you see the rider?'

'Nah. Reckon old Jasper gave us a bum steer,' said Ben.

The two deputies continued their rounds. The town clock struck nine.

Halfway along South Street the sound of a gunshot brought them up sharp. Ben turned to his colleague.

'Where'd that come from?'

'Main Street?' suggested Clay.

Ben sprinted in that direction, Clay followed five paces behind.

Three more shots rang out as Ben turned the corner into Main Street. Four men ran out of the Cattleman's Bank amidst a fusillade of gunfire.

Ben noticed one robber leaning hard against the wall to the side of the bank's front door; another came round the corner of the building at the gallop; his bandanna had slipped down. He wore a black ten-gallon hat, and had a drooping moustache; he was leading a string of horses.

Dust swirled as the bank robbers tried to mount their horses. A bank guard emerged from the doorway of the bank, six-gun in hand; he didn't see the robber behind him. The robber on the stoop shot the guard in the back, then leaped for cover behind a horse trough.

Ben dropped to one knee, still more than one hundred yards from the bank. He raised the shotgun before realizing that the weapon would do little damage at that range. Ben cursed himself profanely for preferring the shotgun to a Winchester. Clay slid alongside.

'Rifle,' Ben shouted. The young deputy threw the Winchester to his senior. Ben took careful aim and fired, one of the bank robbers went down clutching his chest.

'Take cover.' Ben shouted as one by one the robbers managed to get their feet into their stirrups. The outlaw behind the horse trough raised his rifle and fired shot after shot to cover the flight of his cohorts. Ben squeezed off one more shot before scrambling for better cover.

★　★　★

At the far end of North Street Sheriff Jeff Jackson had just said goodbye to his wife when the harsh sound of gunfire drifted along the street. It didn't take two seconds for him to realize what was happening.

'Keep the kids indoors,' he yelled to Laurie as he made for the street, Winchester in one hand, six-gun in the other.

At the corner he saw Ben and Clay. Ben saw him and pointed towards the bank, holding up five fingers.

Only two of the bank robbers had managed to quiet and mount their excited horses. Spooked by the deafening gunfire the other horses reared, whinnied, and milled about nervously. Eventually four robbers were mounted and spurring away. Jeff and Ben opened up with Winchesters; Clay loosed off a couple of shots with his six-gun.

A horse went down with a scream, spilling its rider on to the dusty roadway. Another of the robbers turned his horse when he saw what had happened; he reached out a hand to help his comrade leap up behind him. The fallen outlaw got to his feet, grabbed the horse's bridle, drew his gun and shot his would-be rescuer in the face at point-blank range before pulling him from the saddle. The outlaw leaped into the saddle and raced away in a northerly direction.

Jeff took aim and squeezed the trigger of the Winchester. His bullet slammed into the timber horse trough, sending splinters of wood flying. The robber moved from one side of the horse trough to the other, keeping up a steady rate of fire. Seeing one of his two fallen colleagues move, he doubled his rate of fire, keeping the lawmen's heads down. He shouted to the man to crawl over behind the trough, then the two men sent round after round of hot lead at Jeff and his deputies.

The stand-off dragged on, with both sides swapping harmless shots.

Jeff held up a hand. 'Cease fire,' he shouted to his deputies. For a moment all went deathly quiet. Jeff tied a handkerchief to his Winchester and waved it in the air. The bank robbers stopped firing.

'You two men,' he called out. 'Can you hear me?'

'We hear you,' yelled back Jack Stowe. 'What's on your mind?'

'This makes no sense,' Jeff shouted. 'There's no escape. Give yourselves up. We won't shoot.'

'How do we know you won't plug us?'

'You have my word.'

'Who are you?'

'Sheriff Jeff Jackson.'

'Let's see you, then.'

Ben grabbed Jeff's arm. 'Don't show yourself, Jeff.'

Jeff shook off Ben's hand and stood up slowly. 'Throw down your weapons and come out from behind that horse trough.'

Jack Stowe raised his body into a crouch and took aim, but before he could fire, a single shot from Ben North's Winchester rang out, breaking the unnerving silence, sending the robber's body spinning round wildly before it crashed backwards across the stoop into the wall of the bank.

Three robbers were down, but three had got clean away.

The town was eerily quiet as Jeff walked across the dusty street, thumbing shells into his Winchester.

Ben walked over to the third robber. He pushed a boot under the body, flipping it over.

'This one's dead.'

'This one's dead too, Sheriff,' called out Sid Larkin, one of the bank tellers, pointing to the robber on the stoop. He gestured to the open bank door. 'Three dead inside the bank.'

Jeff looked down at the third outlaw. Half the man's face had been shot away. He was still alive.

'You're dying,' Jeff said coldly. 'Tell me your name and those of your friends and I'll see you get a Christian burial.'

The man's eyes begged for compassion; he tried to speak but his words were drowned out by the blood filling his mouth.

Jeff laid down the Winchester as Doctor Hollis reached his side.

'Do what you can for him, Doc. I need to know who these fellers are.'

Hollis nodded. He mopped away the blood. The man coughed up more.

'Water,' he managed to say. Somebody handed the doctor a ladle of water. He poured some into the man's mouth, inducing more coughing.

'Who was it?' Jeff demanded.

'Paulsons,' the man coughed out. 'Paulson broth . . . ' He died with the name on his lips.

'Paulson Brothers? We got papers on them, ain't we?' asked Ben.

Jeff nodded.

Sid Larkin came out of the bank. 'Sheriff. Hank's still alive.'

They left the outlaw and ran into the bank. Doctor Hollis took over the care of Hank, the assistant manager. The wounded man was propped against a wall; blood covered his shirt and coat. Doc Hollis turned to Jeff.

'He'll live,' he observed. He turned back to the wounded man. 'Bullet missed all your vitals,' he pronounced. 'You are one lucky son of a gun.'

Hank smiled weakly. 'It was the Paulson brothers, Jeff. All three of 'em, with some other dude. I seen a Wanted poster on 'em last time I was in Gallatin City.' He coughed hard, which made him grimace with pain.

'Take it easy,' the doctor told him.

139

Hank recovered and continued. 'They burst in just as we opened up, forced Bart to open the safe. Took the money. Shot Bart. Nobody had time to do anything. It all happened so quickly.'

Jeff grunted and turned to Ben. 'You and Clay organize a posse,' he told him, then shouted, 'Somebody fetch my horse.'

Ben looked around. 'Where is Clay, anyhow?'

Across the street a group of townsfolk crowded round a prostrate figure.

'Over here, Doc,' someone shouted, 'It's Clay Boothe.'

Ben raced across the street, beating Jeff by some yards. He knelt and bent his head forward. Jeff arrived at his side. Blood covered Clay's shirt; it didn't look good.

Doctor Hollis arrived, out of breath. He leaned over the young deputy as Clay recovered consciousness. Clay screamed and writhed, both hands clutching at his stomach. Blood oozed between his white fingers.

'Hold his arms,' Doc Hollis ordered.

Two men sprang forward. The doctor cut away Clay's blood-soaked shirt and examined the wound. All the time Clay was screaming for help. Doc Hollis looked from Jeff to Ben and shook his head.

Ben slumped against the pavement, one hand grabbing for the hitching post.

'He's gone,' called out the doctor. 'It's a mercy,' he added resignedly.

A shock of disbelief jolted through the crowd.

Old Jasper came up with Atlas, the big black, saddled and ready, and with Ajax, on a halter.

Jeff rose, squeezing Ben's shoulder. He mounted Atlas.

'Jeff!'

Jeff recognized his wife's shout.

Laurie ran to him holding his saddle-bags, a gunny sack and a canteen of water.

'Food,' she said.

Jeff leaned down and kissed her hard on the lips. He knew she wanted him to quit the job, but he also knew she supported his pride in not being able to be a quitter.

Jeff straightened up. 'Ben!' he shouted.

Ben got a grip on his emotions.

'Organize that posse,' Jeff told him. 'I'll mark the trail.' He pulled Atlas's rein to wheel the horse, waved to Laurie and spurred away. She blew a kiss, praying for his safe homecoming.

Ben stood up, shouting, 'Who's with me?'

Several men stepped forward.

'OK. Get your guns and horses, food and water. Enough for a few days. Bring some for me. Meet in front of the jail in thirty minutes.' He glanced sideways. 'Doc, will you see to Clay?'

Doctor Hollis nodded.

18

Yellowstone Valley

When Jeff first kicked Atlas into a gallop he was entirely confident of catching up with the bank robbers despite their head start. Atlas was fast and had good staying power. However, now he was not so sure.

At the crossroads five miles northwest of White Bluff Jeff halted to examine the ground and the perplexing multitude of hoofprints. He knew the direction the bank robbers had taken out of town, but reckoned they wouldn't stay on the road long. He tried to put himself in their shoes. Which way would he turn if he were they, he asked himself. Surely not north where the terrain was roughest, or east, his logical brain told him. The Sioux had been active recently to the east of the Yellowstone Valley, the robbers must know that. Nor was it likely they'd head west along the Yellowstone River and run the risk of running into a cavalry patrol out of Fort Ellis. South would take them across the open prairie to the Circle-B ranch. Jeff didn't believe they would risk being in open country. No, their best option would be south-west, he'd put money on it. Guessing *where* they would turn was the real problem; there were any number of trails leading in that direction.

At Thompson's Ferry crossroads, a loud hail drifted across the Yellowstone River. Jeff turned. Old man Thompson was hauling his flat-bottomed ferry across the river towards the southern bank. Jeff waved to him. The only passenger was a travelling pedlar and his wife.

'Mornin', Sheriff,' Thompson greeted as he tied up the ferry.

The pedlar drove his two-horse team down the ramp, handed over the fare, and called out '*adios*'.

'I'm chasing three men. Robbed the bank this morning,' Jeff told him. 'Seen any riders?'

Old man Thompson rubbed his whiskered chin. 'Come to think of it, I did see riders. I was over on the other bank, jest dropped off a coupla sorry-lookin' drifters. Tekin' a relief behind them trees, you might say,' He pointed enthusiastically. 'Well, sir — '

Jeff butted in. 'How many riders?'

Thompson looked irked to have his story so rudely interrupted. 'Oh. I don' know, Sheriff. There was at least three of 'em, I guess. Plus a coupla loose horses.'

'That must have been them. Which way they head?'

Thompson spat on the ground. 'Ah'd say they was headed up the old Bozeman trail.'

'Towards Fort Ellis?'

'S'what I said.'

'Thanks.' In a trice Jeff was back in the saddle, racing away. He was still not able to believe the Paulsons would take the trail west, but old man Thompson had been certain.

Spring and summer had been warm but uncommonly dry that year. Fall had announced its arrival with a bang; storms, sudden cloudbursts. Surprisingly it hadn't rained for several days until the previous night, when a freak cloudburst had soaked the land. Rivers rose dangerously as water cascaded across bone-hard ground too hard to allow much seepage.

A few miles further on, at the next crossroads, Jeff reined in Ajax and dismounted, scouring the stony ground. It took some time before he saw what he was looking for. The tracks of more than three horses. He knelt down to take a closer look. Some of the tracks were deeper than others, he was sure there were three sets of these heavier tracks — three bank robbers, plus maybe two riderless horses.

The tracks cut south across the Fort Ellis road, swinging south-west towards Boulder Valley, a place Jeff knew well.

He watered Ajax and Atlas at a small stream, took a drink himself, and bit into one of the sandwiches Laurie had made, figuring the Paulsons wouldn't be able to keep up the galloping pace too much longer, not unless they had fresh horses staked out and waiting. He shook his head, not wanting to concede the possibility.

Ten minutes later he was back in the saddle, holding down Ajax's pace, figuring this chase would most likely be a long haul. The young horse seemed to understand he was pursuing a gang of criminals, he chomped at the bit, wanting to run faster.

Jeff tugged on the reins. 'Boulder Valley,' he said out loud. 'Come on, horse. Time for a short cut.'

Jeff turned off the road on to the less well used side trail leading to Snake Pass. He followed the rising trail for several miles through steep-sided hills, then, when the climb grew steeper, swapped horses for a few miles before moving back to Ajax.

147

He set Ajax at the steep slope that faced them and urged the younger horse forward, feeling the raw power of the animal under him.

The rewarding panoramic view from the crest of the hill offered a magnificent 360 degrees. He looked at the line of distant peaks. This was his country, and he knew it well. Knew almost every blade of grass, every stream, river and creek, every stark cliff of black volcanic rock, every sandy draw and steep arroyo.

Jeff urged his horse forward, moving carefully, his sharp eyes scouting the wild undulating terrain ahead for the slightest hint of movement. He kicked Ajax into a canter as the crest flattened out a little; the trail swung a degree or two north. At the point of the crest Jeff dismounted, fed the horses, and took a drink of water.

He ferreted around in his saddlebags for his old army telescope. He raised it to his eye and slowly scanned the distant valley floor. Disappointed, he was about to fold the scope when he saw what looked like a small cloud of dust. He watched the cloud for some minutes to make certain it was what he thought it was: only a group of horses could kick up that much dust. But was it the robbers, or a small herd of mustangs?

One more swift glance convinced Jeff it was the bank robbers, and they were heading towards the three finger canyons on the west side of Boulder Valley.

He turned Ajax due south towards Snake Pass. If he was figuring right, the short cut through the pass would see him gain a lot of time, always providing the Paulsons would cooperate and keep to the main track south along the valley floor.

The old trail through Snake Pass was not well used. Thick strands of brush and sage had grown across the track. Ajax stepped around the obstacles as nimbly as could be expected from such an intelligent animal.

As he breasted the crest of a rise Jeff

shielded his eyes and searched the land stretching away to his right, hoping for a glimpse of a dust cloud, but there was nothing. Had he guessed wrong? he wondered. He kicked Ajax into a canter and rode along the crest; a gentle breeze was fanning the leaves of the trees.

Jeff halted at a fine vantage point he knew, dismounted at the top of a dry, shallow, sandy wash and took out the telescope. Resting it on a rock he scanned the valley floor for a second time.

Through the heat haze on the opposite side of the valley he thought he caught sight of some movement. Was it the Paulsons? Was it anything? A long dense stand of cedar and spruce concealed the area he was looking at. No other movement came to his eye. Had he imagined it? He pushed back his hat and grimaced in disappointment.

A second look rewarded him with the distant sight of what he decided were three riders, plus a couple of loose horses going hell for leather.

Jeff's heart sank as he realized he had guessed wrong. Now catching up with them was less likely than he had originally thought. He wouldn't even come close. The Paulsons hadn't taken the south road along the valley as Jeff had figured; they had veered west towards Sulphur Springs and Beartooth Pass. Jeff left a marker for Ben and the posse to follow, and changed horses, cursing as he resigned himself to the fact that his wrong decision would cost him a few hours. Well, moping about it wouldn't do any good.

Finding the easy trail to the valley floor would eat more precious time. He decided to go straight for it.

Leaving the Snake Pass trail behind, Jeff recklessly set Atlas at the steep rock strewn slope that would lead him directly down to the valley floor. There was no track or trail, just loose shale and stones. Atlas slid and blew hard; behind him Ajax whinnied in protest, as horses and rider struggled down the slope. On a small flat area halfway down the slope Jeff halted Atlas; the worst part of the descent was now behind them. He dismounted out of breath, legs shaking. Atlas gave him a stern look of disapproval.

Neither man nor horse would want to attempt such a foolhardy descent again.

After resting for a few moments Jeff moved his saddle to Ajax and now rode in more of a zigzag pattern until the ground levelled out at the foot of the slope.

The place where he had seen the outlaws was hidden by the undulating terrain, but Jeff had made sure to mark the direction in his mind and spurred Ajax into a fast run. He forded Pitchers Creek and the much faster-flowing water of the Boulder River, thankful that neither proved to be difficult, although Ajax did stumble once, almost pitching his rider into the water. Through the trees he spotted the trail to Beartooth Pass, leading eventually to the high peaks of the Absaroka mountain range.

He soon found a number of recognizable hoofprints that could only have been made by one group of riders: the Paulsons.

His quarry must have to slow down soon, at least Jeff hoped so. A number of broken twigs and trampled down grass told him he was on the right track. He switched mounts again, intent on keeping his horses as fresh as possible.

$$\star \quad \star \quad \star$$

The voice was loud and commanding. 'I'm swearin' you all in as deputies. Raise your right hands.' The six volunteers did as Deputy Ben North ordered. Ben read the words of the oath. Then, satisfied, he added, 'Thank you all for volunteering.'

'I got two packhorses loaded and ready,' the hostler told Ben.

'Thanks.' Ben meticulously checked the supplies.

Doctor Hollis led his horse alongside Ben's.

'Whoa, Doc,' Ben said loudly, 'you ain't comin'.'

The doctor's face was filled with misunderstanding. He laughed nervously. 'You are joking, right?'

'No. Somebody needs to stay in town to look after the wounded. Keep the law. That's you, *amigo*. I need you to stay in White Bluff.' Without waiting for a response, Ben turned to the others. 'OK, let's go. Follow me.'

The six members of the posse trailed behind their leader: seven remounts and two packhorses on halters brought up the rear.

Picking up Jeff's well marked trail through Snake Pass was easy until they reached the point where Jeff had chanced the steep escarpment. Recognizing the level of horsemanship of his posse Ben led them further along the old trail to a point where a side trail snaked to the valley floor far below. Ben soon found Jeff's trail and headed the posse towards the foothills.

19

Three Forks Canyon

'Horses comin' slow and easy.' Abe
Paulson pointed. 'Down that side
canyon.'

'Take cover behind them rocks,'
Webb Paulson told his brother. 'Zeke.
You get over there.'

Minutes later two riders rode out of
the canyon into the small clearing: an
Indian boy and a girl.

Zeke Paulson spurred his horse into
the path of the newcomers. He caught
the bridle of the girl's pony, and
manoeuvred his own horse to box in
the other. Abe grabbed the boy's pony's
bridle.

Zeke let out a high-pitched whistle.
'Well. Lookee what we got here.' He
spurred his horse alongside. 'What's
your name, girlie?' He reached out a

hand trying to stroke her long hair.

Sarah shied away from Zeke's grubby fingers, saying nothing.

Jason took in the situation at a glance: three armed desperadoes. He knew he needed to get help.

'Don't you like me, darlin'?' Zeke turned to his brothers. 'Check 'er out. Phewee. Ain't she sumpthin'?'

Sarah felt his lustful eyes take in every inch of her.

'Purty li'l thing, ain't you?' Zeke reached for her again. 'Wha's'amarra, cat got your tongue?'

'Zeke!' shouted Abe. 'She's an Injun.'

Zeke looked surprised.

'She's an Injun,' Abe shouted again. 'Can't you see?'

Zeke looked at each of his brothers then back to Sarah. 'Well, she sure is a purty one.' Zeke Paulson had never been the sharpest knife in the drawer, but he rounded on his brother. 'Abe. If'n she's an Injun, why's she wearing white-woman's duds?'

'How the hell do I know?' Abe

157

drawled. 'What your name, honey?'

Sarah had had enough. 'You ruffians had better let us go or it will go hard for you.'

'Whoa, hoss,' cried a surprised Zeke. 'You're sure ascarin' me.'

Sarah ignored his sarcasm. 'Come here,' she whispered to Zeke, beckoning with her finger. Zeke leaned towards her, hoping to hear a word of encouragement. 'Closer,' she whispered.

Zeke bent his head. Sarah kicked her left leg as high and hard as she could; catching Zeke on the nose. He slumped from the saddle as Sarah wrenched the bridle out of his grip. Webb Paulson looked on unconcerned as Sarah urged her pony into a gallop. Then he drew his big Sharps carbine, aimed and fired one shot. Sarah pitched headlong on to the sandy ground, her pony dead beside her. Webb dismounted.

Jason shouted, heads turned. Jason looked up at the cliff face and pointed. Abe Paulson's grip on the bridle relaxed a tad as his eyes searched the spot where Jason was pointing. That was all Jason needed; he tugged back hard on the reins causing both horses to rear. Abe dragged his hand clear as Jason kicked back his heels. His pony lurched into a gallop, racing around the jutting rock formation at the mouth of the canyon in the direction of White Bluff, dust and stones flying from the pony's hoofs.

Abe gave chase, knowing the chance of catching the fleet-footed pony was hopeless.

'Let 'im go,' Webb shouted. 'We got the girl.'

Abe ignored his brother and drew his six-gun, squeezing off a couple of shots in rapid succession. The bullets whined as they ricocheted harmlessly from rock to rock, missing their intended target by some distance.

'Don't waste bullets!' yelled Webb.

Reluctantly Abe holstered his side-iron.

Three Forks Canyon split into three

separate trails. Jason had sped away down the canyon towards White Bluff. The Paulsons took the northern trail.

'Get her up on one of them loose horses,' Webb ordered. 'Tie her hands to the saddle pommel.'

'What good's the girl?' asked Abe.

'Insurance,' said Webb. 'Zeke, you watch that wild-cat real good.'

Zeke rubbed his nose. 'That won't be hard, bro. She's right purty.'

'Keep your hands off her till I say different.'

'Aw, Webb. That ain't gon'be no fun.'

★ ★ ★

Jeff followed along a game trail dotted with a few straggly fir trees and low juniper bushes. One weary minute succeeded another as Jeff followed the tracks of the three man procession. Half an hour was lost when he was forced to cast around on a patch of stony ground for signs of the riders he sought. Then he found what he believed was a spot where a metal horseshoe had chipped away a piece of rock and he was off again. He swung Atlas around a stand of firs on to a steeply rising narrowing trail.

Jeff stared up at the rock face. No sense in looking at it, he told himself. He spurred Atlas into the climb, constantly patting the horse's neck and flanks to encourage the animal when the big black protested.

At the top of the climb neither of Jeff's horses needed much of an invitation to munch at the green carpet of grass around them. Jeff paused only a few minutes, then urged his horse forward.

Atlas's ears pricked, Ajax too reacted to something. Aside from wind stirring the leaves in the trees, Jeff heard nothing, but respected the heightened senses of his animals. He eased back on the reins, unsure what had caused the horses to react.

Jeff's throat was dry, he needed a drink of water. He shielded his eyes from the glare of the sun and peered across a meadow dotted with a myriad of different grasses and wild flowers stretching out in front of him. The shallow banks on either side of a wide, fast-flowing stream were luxuriant with verdant growth. Jeff took off his hat and wiped his sweaty face and neck with his bandanna then dismounted, the material of his shirt sticking to his sweaty back. Tugging at the seat of his pants, he led Atlas and Ajax down the gently sloping embankment. The big horses whinnied, and began cropping the grass, pausing only to take a drink from a small eddy. Shadows of leaves dappled horses and rider, the semi-shade bringing a degree of cool comfort after the heat of the valley floor.

Jeff lifted his canteen from the saddle horn, emptied the contents and dipped the canteen in the stream. He sat on a rock and took a long pull at the cool refreshing liquid, then refilled the canteen. The shelter of a tall blue spruce provided a welcome respite;

there was no question of turning back in his mind, but doubts had set in. A few minutes' rest was all he was going to allow himself.

After a couple of minutes he mounted Ajax, urging the young horse into a canter along the pretty pasture, passing a couple of cows branded with the Double-J. Some others lifted their heads to watch the interloper; most ignored the tall rider crossing their terrain.

For a good few miles the gradient rose steadily. In several places along the trail the tracks of ten or so cows mingled with clear imprints of shod horses; the tracks disappeared over a patch of harsh rock-strewn terrain.

After another hour's hard ride from Snake Pass Jeff reined in his horse on the crest of a tree-fringed ridge; the view in every direction was magnificent. He felt his heart pound that little bit faster as he gazed with pride at the lush green valley below. This was Jackson land, as far as the eye could see; paid for, signed, sealed and delivered.

He gazed west to the far-off hills, recognizing the distant rock formations. He remembered every detail of each one. The natural features of the Three Finger Canyon where, five years ago, Clem, Dan and he had built corrals.

Straight ahead a strip of shining silver marked the passage of Boulder Brook, sparkling amidst the verdant landscape, snaking its way east from the foothills of the Absaroka Mountains to join the Boulder River.

Jeff set his mount into a headlong dash for the spot. Not wanting to lose time, he rode recklessly fast down the steep hillside. Although it was much less steep than the earlier one, more than once he felt his horse almost stumble.

Panting hard Jeff reined in at the foot of the steep embankment. He took off his bandanna and wiped the sweat from his eyes. He blew out a big breath and tugged his shirt away from his sweaty back, then dismounted, he moved his saddle to Atlas.

A stand of tall firs grew on a small rise on one side of a natural cleft in the land. The centre of the cleft was reasonably flat. Behind the trees the rocky outcrop he had seen earlier stood solid and imposing. A sparkling stream ran near by.

*   *   *

Ben North's posse made slower progress than Jeff, but that didn't stop one or two members complaining about the stiff pace being set. Eventually Ben was forced to accept the need for some food and he called a temporary halt to the chase. A camp was quickly set up in a clearing by a gurgling brook. They soon got a fire going, and even Ben had to admit he enjoyed the hot bacon and beans, washed down with strong coffee.

With food inside them the posse made a much happier start into the foothills, leaving the relatively flat land behind.

* * *

The galloping pony seemed almost to fly around the stand of blue spruce. Hearing the sound of fast approaching hoofbeats Jeff reined in Ajax. He reached forward and drew the Winchester from the saddle holster, clicking a shell into place with mechanical precision.

He was surprised to see who the rider was.

'Jason!' he shouted, edging Ajax into the open. 'Jason!'

Jason's pony skidded to a halt in a flurry of dust when the rider recognized who had shouted his name.

The boy was out of breath and was sweating profusely. 'Jeff!' he called out, equally surprised to see the sheriff.

'Where are you heading in such an all-fired hurry?' Jeff asked, sliding the Winchester back inside the scabbard.

'Bilitaachiia. Sorry. I mean Sarah. Three men have taken her.'

Jeff wasn't certain he'd heard correctly. 'What is it you are telling me?'

'Three men have taken Sarah. My sister,' Jason added irritatedly.

'Where was this?'

'Three Forks Canyon.'

'When?'

'Just now. I managed to get away. Need to get help.'

'Help is here,' Jeff told him confidently. 'Can you describe the men?'

Jason did his best to give a description of the kidnappers.

'The Paulson brothers,' Jeff said out loud. 'They just robbed the Cattleman's Bank in White Bluff. It's them I'm trailing. Posse's behind me.'

He considered the alternatives for a moment, then said, 'Show me.'

They reached Three Forks Canyon an hour or so after noon.

Angry buzzards scattered as Jeff stepped down from Atlas's back. A few hopped back towards the corpse of a dead pony, eyeing the two people who had interrupted their lunch with hate-filled eyes.

'Sarah's pony,' explained Jason. 'One

167

of the men shot him.'

Jeff ground-hitched his horses and walked the area, examining the mêlée of hoofprints. The tracks were plain to read. Two riders had travelled along the southern canyon, as Jason had said.

'Jason. Ride back to Red Hawk's camp. Get him to send braves round Bute Mountain to meet me at Sulphur Springs. I'll wait there.'

'I'll be with them,' Jason promised.

'OK, get going.'

'Good luck.' Jason called out. 'See you at Sulphur Springs.' The teenager's words echoed down the canyon.

So, the Paulsons had taken a hostage. That was a complication that needed careful factoring into the equation. Jeff figured he would have time to eat something before starting the climb that would take him to Sulphur Springs.

He lit a fire and quickly cooked up some beans and coffee.

Jeff kicked soil over the embers and stamped out any sparks that lingered.

Next he cut two long branches, tied them in a cross and pushed the sharpened bases well into the soft earth. He wrote a short note to Ben telling him what had happened and asking him to follow at speed. Jeff secured the note to the cross.

The northern fork of the canyon rose steadily to a narrow high pass, impassable in winter, barely passable for four months of the year. Once through the pass the going would be easier as the trail led to a large expanse of flat pastureland. Jeff had been there many times, it was part of the land owned by him and his kin. He wondered if the Paulsons were heading for the old line shack on the flats, and whether they had put fresh horses there.

That the bank robbers already had a number of remounts was in their favour, but Jeff knew they would need them once they hit the snowline.

For several miles Jeff rode through high-walled canyons. The booming sound of rushing water assailed his ears as he entered an open area. A fast-flowing stream cascaded over smooth rocks, sending columns of spray high into the air. A deep canyon branched off to the north. Jeff dismounted and squatted by the trail, scanning his memory for information about this place. He remembered the canyon ended in a sheer rock face. Ahead, the going would be considerably tougher — and colder, he reminded himself, as the trail rose steeply towards Beartooth Pass.

Earlier, what sign there was had been easy to follow from the saddle, but now the tracks were muddied and confused. At the foot of the slope the trail crossed a small tree-lined valley before skirting a tiny alkali lake. A dense wall of pines at the far end of the canyon appeared to present a solid impenetrable barrier. Jeff recalled that the trail broke through the wall of trees, actually winding through and between the big pines.

Ajax and Atlas's hoofs crunched over a carpet of pine needles. Branches fluttered in the light wind. A chute of water cascaded out from a cleft high in the towering rock face in front of him, dropping into a pool that would eventually feed the lake. A myriad of bubbles broke the surface to pervade the air with the putrid stink of sulphur. He had arrived at Sulphur Springs.

Jeff dismounted and fed Atlas and Ajax; the supply of oats was running out. Both horses munched away happily, drinking deeply from a tiny stream of crystal-clear mountain water before moving to crop at the sweet green grass when the oats were finished. He stretched out his long legs, then settled his back against a smooth rock and waited patiently for Red Hawk and his braves. The rest was very welcome, allowing him and his horses to recover a little from their arduous journey.

A chill wind fanned Jeff's cheek. He looked to the west, concerned that the sky over the Absaroka range was dark; in places it was coal black: bad weather was coming in. Not good, he thought. He wondered if High Pass was open. It should be; heavy snowfall wasn't expected for a couple of months.

After waiting impatiently for nearly an hour Jeff decided to press on. He reckoned it was fair to assume that Jason had delivered his message to Red Hawk, but that something had prevented the braves from reaching Sulphur Springs.

Jeff drew signs on the hard earth and cut a sign into the bark of a tree at the side of the trail. He put on his coat, saddled Ajax, mounted and set off at an even pace.

20

The trail below Beartooth Pass

'Weather's closin' in,' Abe Paulson observed. 'Weren't like this a week ago.'

Light snow began to fall, blanketing the hard ground with a coating of powder.

Horses blew and snorted as their hoofs dragged through the frozen grass; they stepped slowly and cautiously, nervously sensing the chance of slipping.

'We need to find shelter,' said Zeke.

'That's where we're heading, ain't it?' Webb muttered sarcastically.

'How far you reckon?' Zeke asked, rubbing at the thin coating of frost forming on his lips.

'Can't be more'n ten miles to that old line shack where we left the remounts,' snapped Webb.

'When we gonna count the money?' Zeke asked.

'Later!' Webb thundered.

Undeterred, Zeke asked, 'How much you reckon we got?'

'Shut up!' Webb told him.

Zeke shivered and went into a silent sulk. Deep down he hated his oldest brother.

A huge snow cloud rose skyward in the distance, followed by the crashing boom of an avalanche.

'Webb,' Abe whispered. Webb turned. 'Someone's coming up the trail behind us,' Abe told him. 'One rider, two horses, as far as I kin make out.'

'Where?'

Abe pointed into the swirling snow to a spot down below. 'Long way down. Beyond that outcrop of rock.'

'How far back?'

'Good coupla hours at least. 'Specially now it's started snowin'.' Abe rubbed some warmth into his half-frozen fingers. 'You sure Beartooth Pass'll be open?'

'You better pray it is,' Webb snarled.

Abe peered back down the trail, but the lone rider had disappeared.

'Webb. You think anyone from town might be trailin' us?'

'How the heck do I know?' Webb growled. 'Why? You figure that rider's from town?'

Abe shrugged. 'Could be.'

'Well, whoever it is he'll be slowed right down by this weather. Come on, let's get movin'.' Webb Paulson spurred his horse onward.

The higher they climbed the colder it got, the air temperature falling sharply. The snow fell more heavily.

After half an hour Zeke came out of his sulk. 'How much longer to the line shack?' he asked.

'Quit your moanin',' Webb ordered. 'How's that squaw doin'?'

'I ain't moanin'. Jest askin',' Zeke protested. He looked across at Sarah; only the red tip of her nose was visible under the blanket covering her head. 'She's OK.' Zeke called back. 'Ain't you, honey?' he said to Sarah, pulling the collar of his coat tighter. Sarah stared straight ahead.

'Keep a tight grip on that halter,' shouted Webb.

Zeke edged his mount closer to his brother. 'Abe. *Abe.*' His voice was almost a whisper; he didn't want Webb to hear.

Abe turned his head.

'What you gonna do with your share?' Zeke enquired.

'Webb told you to shut up about the money,' Abe growled, 'so shut up, or me'n Webb'll shut you up.'

Zeke dropped back, finally getting the message, but failing to understand his brother's lack of curiosity about the money.

The wind veered, now blowing freezing sleet and snow directly into their faces. Horses slowed, hoofs dragging through the deepening snow. The cold was intense, their fingers and toes began to lose sensation.

Webb turned. 'We need to find some shelter till this thing blows over.'

'I just said that,' Zeke replied.

'Shut up. I'm thinkin'.' Webb Paulson scanned the trail ahead. Seeing nothing suitable he said, 'We'll go back to that cleft in the rocks we just passed. Looked a likely spot for a cave.' Ignoring his brother's response, he turned his horse and led the way back down the trail.

On close inspection the narrow cleft in the rocks revealed a deep dark cave, the entrance just wide enough for a horse to pass through.

Zeke pushed Sarah against a wall and threw another blanket to her.

'Find some wood and kindlin', get a fire goin',' ordered Webb.

The cave brightened with the welcome flames, shadows dancing across cold rock. Steam rose from damp clothing as Abe put on a pot of coffee.

Zeke handed a tin plate of beans to Sarah. She folded her arms and turned her face away.

'You gotta eat sumpthin',' he told her. She ignored his advice. 'Suit yourself,' he muttered.

Sarah shivered under the blankets. She was cold and hungry, but was determined not to show any weakness. Long ago she had decided not to complain or to make herself a burden to these men in case they decided to harm her. She knew these mountains better than they did, that much was quite obvious, and sooner or later there would be a chance to escape.

The firelight cast a grotesque show on the walls of the cave. Somewhere in the distant foothills coyotes began a howling contest.

Ignoring her earlier response, Zeke Paulson ladled a few beans on to a tin plate, then ambled over to Sarah.

'Here. You better eat sumpthin'.'

'I told you before, I'm not hungry,' she said defiantly.

'Suit yourself. Like I told you before.' Zeke grinned, like a child, aping what Sarah had said.

A strong breeze gusted into the cave, fanning the flames of the fire, stirring the branches on the pines and juniper bushes at the mouth of the cave.

Abe and Zeke kept the fire burning from the good supply of dry wood at the back of the cave. The horses settled down once they had been fed and watered.

Night set in. The Paulsons settled down. Soon all three were snoring loudly. Sarah rubbed the bonds that bound her hands against the sharpest edge of rock that she could find. Her legs and feet had been tied, a strand of rope was hooked around Zeke's arm.

After half an hour or so of rubbing, the sound of rope strands snapping echoed softly through the cave. Sarah's wrists were red raw, her swollen fingers almost lifeless.

She made several attempts to undo the tight knots binding her legs and feet, but her chilled fingers were too numb to make much progress. As silently as she could she slid slowly closer to the fire. Zeke stirred and snuffled, then began to snore again.

Sarah held her hands to the fire, feeling a degree of warmth returning. She saw there were a few beans left in the pan; she devoured the tepid food with gusto.

The blade of Zeke's hunting knife

protruded a little from a decorated sheath. Reflecting the firelight it drew her eyes to the possibility of escape. She eased closer, her trembling fingers reaching for the handle. Slowly she withdrew the blade, scared to make even the slightest sudden movement. Then suddenly the blade came free and she tightened her fingers round the handle. She began to saw through the rope binding her feet. The shadow of her movement was bold upon the cave wall.

Free at last of her bonds Sarah eased her legs, realizing the futility of attempting to stand until she had massaged some life back into her muscles. She rubbed her legs until her hands and fingers ached.

Sarah struggled unsteadily to her feet. Pulling one of the blankets around her she steadied herself with a hand on the cave wall. The rock was slippery and slimy. On more than one occasion she almost fell, but got away with only grazing her knee.

At the cave entrance she peered out

in dismay. Snow was still falling heavily. A drift two or three feet high had built up to block the entrance. A howling wind tore at the blanket, a flurry of snow borne on the wind crashed into her face. There was no escape on foot.

Her terrified mind went into a panic-fuelled turmoil; she knew her feet, if not the whole of her body, would be frozen long before she could get below the snowline; she wasn't dressed for this kind of severe weather. She cursed her luck and made her way back to the fire.

A couple of the horses eyed her suspiciously. Sarah looked back at them, her brain working overtime. Even if she could get a horse past the sleeping desperadoes there was no way a horse could make it through snow that deep.

She threw a couple of logs on to the fire and watched the sparks spiral high above her head. Suddenly realizing how cold she was she grabbed the other blanket and sat by the fire, her knees raised, her hands and head resting on them forlornly. The heat burnt the soles of her boots and her hair until she was forced to draw back from the flames. She lay down and fell into an exhausted sleep.

Sarah woke to the appetizing smell of bacon frying. She raised her head, then tried to lift a hand to brush a strand of hair from her eyes. Her hands were tied, a knotted loop held her legs and feet securely.

'Mornin', darlin'.' Zeke smiled. 'Go for a nice walk last night?'

Sarah looked around. The horses were saddled. Abe was fastening the cinch on one animal. He turned and grinned at her. Webb sat on the other side of the fire, his face dark as thunder.

Abe stood at the cave entrance, peering out. 'Snow's melting,' he informed everyone.

The temperature had risen considerably since the sun had broken over the rim of the eastern mountains.

'Grub's ready,' Zeke called out, 'come'n get it.' He swung round to Sarah. 'You want some?'

21

The trail to Beartooth Pass

Jeff looked up at the snow-filled sky, not looking forward one bit to the next part of the journey. He shrugged off the negative thought. Once through the highest point of the pass the downhill trail would be easy; the worst of the snow would be left behind.

In a sparsely grassed clearing Jeff spied what looked to be a faint hoofprint in the shadow of an overhanging branch. He dismounted; there were many imprints of hoofs, five horses at least. To the side of the trail he saw grass half-sprung back to its normal position, some still lying flat. His quarry couldn't be far ahead.

He walked the horses across the sloping ground beyond a dense screen of firs and blue spruce. The grass grew thicker and stronger here. The meadow was beautiful, a myriad of alpine plants and hardy wild flowers sparkled in the weak sunshine, their blossoms turned toward the light. Wind sang through the branches of the trees. On another day, thought Jeff, this beauty would be like a magnet, not allowing any traveller to pass hastily by.

The deep-red sun began to dip behind the crests of the western mountains, announcing the arrival of dusk and forcing Jeff to halt. Seeing the trail in the growing gloom was proving difficult if not downright dangerous, and the darkening sky was filled with the threat of snow. He decided it would be better to camp now whilst he was still below the snowline, reckoning the fugitives would also have to camp for the night. He didn't envy their chances of staying warm if they made a try for the pass tonight; only a fool would attempt it.

Another consideration was that Atlas was blowing harder than Jeff had ever heard him. He dismounted in a glade and unsaddled the big black horse, remembering how the speed and strength of this horse had saved his life more than once during the war. Ajax looked tired from his stint, Jeff fed and watered both horses. He quickly got a fire going, cooked up some hot food, drank coffee, and worried about Sarah.

She was a tough girl, that much he recognized; having spent a good portion of her life being raised by her Crow Indian relatives. Nonetheless, that didn't calm his fears. The Paulsons were desperate men. Hopefully . . . well, maybe it was better not to go there. He threw down his bedroll and lay down, knowing he was in for an uncomfortable night.

A little nip of something a mite stronger than coffee wouldn't have gone amiss, he reflected, but sadly he hadn't thought to bring any with him. Just as well, Jeff ruminated, recognizing that he might not have been able to stop at one nip.

He flipped the leather thong off the

hammer of his Remington and drew the six-gun, remembering when the six-shooter had still been fairly new; some of the manufacturer's grease had still been on the moving parts when he'd taken it off a dead Confederate major. The gun's superb balance always felt good in his big hand; when he pointed it, it was like an extension of his arm. The feel of the pistol in his hand brought back many memories. He wiped the handgun and checked the action, recalling memories from more recent times. Like the time he and Clem had trailed Alexander Brown into hills not so far from where he lay now.

Jeff closed his eyes and slept.

★　★　★

Jeff woke with a start, his chilled fingers still wrapped tightly around the grip of his Remington. For a few minutes he lay still and silent, waiting for another sound to follow upon the one he thought he'd heard a few seconds earlier. A couple of logs on his fire were still alight, smoke rose toward the night sky. He wouldn't have been able to say how long he stayed in that position, but before he moved the first rays of pale daylight had crept over the eastern mountains. No further sound drifted on the morning air.

Daylight hit the clouds on the eastern horizon. Anxious to get going Jeff breakfasted on water, hardtack biscuit, and beef jerky. It was meagre fare, but adequate in the circumstances. He hoped the fugitives would want something more substantial that needed cooking. Both his horses snorted a protest when Jeff lifted away the nosebags of oats over their heads. He saddled Ajax and climbed into the saddle, easily picking up the trail.

★   ★   ★

Ben North lead the posse into the dusty canyon.

'Here's where Jeff made camp,' he said, and re-read Jeff's note.

'You think we're gaining on him?'

'No way to tell for sure.' Ben replied. 'Come on. Let's pick up the pace. This canyon's only got one trail. Can't be any way else but ahead.' He urged his horse into a fast trot. The others followed.

The hoofbeats of a single horse behind them slowed Ben to a walk. Then he heard the shout.

'Ben! Wait up.'

Ben raised his arm to halt the posse. Clem Jackson came galloping around a curve in a cloud of dust. He reined in alongside Ben's horse.

'Heard what happened,' he said. 'Thought you might appreciate another gun.'

Ben clasped Clem's proffered hand.

'Sure can,' he told the newcomer. Ben quickly brought Clem up to speed as the posse trotted along behind them.

'Right. Let's go, *amigo*,' he said urging his mount into a fast canter.

22

The trail to Beartooth Pass

As the Paulsons approached Beartooth Pass the morning dawned grey, but at least the cold snap seemed to have passed. Water dripped from everywhere as the pale sun melted the snow.

Sarah's wrists hurt almost enough to make her cry out in pain, but she had decided it would be better to say nothing; she was too proud to show any fear to these men. Riding the big horse across the rough ground whilst hanging on to the saddle pommel with both hands was uncomfortable, she found she wasn't able to move her weight in step with the horse as she was able to do when holding the reins of her pony.

As the seemingly endless journey wore on Sarah began to feel the fear inside her growing ever stronger. She didn't know these men. They were all big, except for their obvious leader who was huge. All she knew of them was that they were brothers and bad through and through. Not one had shown the slightest inkling of human kindness.

She feared the youngest of the three most: Zeke, the others called him. He seemed more than a little on the slow side, in some ways more animal than man. He grunted a lot, scratched and rubbed himself to excess in all the most embarrassing places. At every opportunity Zeke had tried to rub himself against her.

She tried not to think what might happen if the huge leader relaxed his control over this man. She was vulnerable and she knew it; she was excessively tired through trying to stay awake, not daring to let slip her guard in case Zeke pounced. Sarah shuddered at the thought. All kinds of horrific images flew into her imagination. Ugh! She shuddered again. Zeke was horrible. Ugly, and he stank like a pigsty.

She needed to find a weapon of some kind with which to defend herself from the feared attentions of this brute.

The leader halted in a bowl-shaped hollow. A stream gurgled down a small slope.

'Water the horses,' Webb Paulson commanded, without nominating who should carry out the task, but Zeke knew his brother meant him.

The younger Paulson dismounted, grabbed Sarah and dumped her unceremoniously on the ground. 'Stay put,' he told her, scratching his crotch.

Zeke led the horses to the stream.

Sarah looked around and back up the trail into the mouth of the narrow canyon through which they had just passed. Seeing nothing to raise her spirits she concentrated on searching for something to use as a weapon. Ideally something sharp, something she could easily conceal. She found nothing suitable other than a small pointed rock; it just about fitted into her hand.

When Zeke returned he threw a

canteen of fresh water to her; it hit her high on the arm.

'Drink!' Zeke ordered.

Sarah drank.

Zeke watched her every movement. Sarah looked away, not wanting to make eye contact.

'Zeke. Come here,' the huge man commanded.

Zeke did as he was told, and the three men began some kind of discussion.

Sarah was hungrier than she had ever been. She tried to listen to their conversation, but their words were difficult to hear above the sound of the wind.

Ten minutes later they were back in the saddle, all except Zeke, who was helping Sarah mount the horse. A big stupid grin spread widely across his face as he pushed her up on to the horse's back, his rough hands touching every part of her body they could. The ordeal ended with a hearty slap on her rump.

Sarah had already made up her mind to kill Zeke at the first opportunity, and suddenly that opportunity presented itself. She swung her rock-filled hand with all her might. Zeke saw the blow coming as he turned his head towards her, a terrified and unbelieving look in his eyes. Instinctively, but too late, he threw up an arm.

The sharp rock crashed into the side of his temple. Blood spurted as he staggered backwards half a pace. Sarah leaned forward and swung her arm a second time, bringing more blood from Zeke's wound.

Zeke's knees gave way and he toppled forward.

Sarah clapped her heels against the horse's flanks sending the bay leaping into a gallop. She gave the horse its head, keeping low to the horse's back whilst she strained to reach the reins streaming in the wind. The animal responded and raced back along the trail towards Beartooth Pass.

The sound of galloping horses came from behind; she knew Zeke's brothers would pursue her. The big horse wasn't the quickest or the most manoeuverable. It struggled to get around the many boulders strewn across the winding switchback trail, skidding more than once round the base of a cliff.

Sarah's heart leaped; she was certain she was pulling away from her pursuers; her horse had much less weight to carry. Also, she had a small head start.

Coming round another sharp turn the horse shied at the wall of rock facing it. Sarah strained on the reins to pull the animal's head to the right, but it wasn't easy with both hands tied together.

'Turn, you stupid animal,' she shouted, and was relieved as, slowly, the horse began to turn.

The horse shook as one of its front legs snapped. Sarah just managed to jump clear as the side of the horse smacked against a protruding rock. The animal let out the scream of a banshee, and lay writhing on the ground.

The breath having been knocked out of her, Sarah gulped in lungfuls of air and struggled to her feet. Sounds of galloping horses assailed her ears. She looked around for somewhere to hide. Seeing nothing but sheer rock walls she broke into a run. Round a turn she sped, pain shooting up her leg from her right ankle; she must have twisted it when she jumped from the horse's back. She began to limp, almost imperceptibly at first, then the limp became more pronounced with each step. She despaired, knowing she couldn't outrun the two riders behind her; they were coming up fast.

Tears of despair filled her eyes as she stopped running. She hobbled over to a flat rock, sat down and put her head in her hands. She sobbed loudly. She had made a break for freedom, but this one hadn't worked any better than the first. Now she would have to face the wrath of her pursuers.

A short way back down the track a single gunshot rang out; she knew instantly what it was. A few moments later Webb and Abe Paulson reined in their panting horses in front of her.

195

Sarah looked up at them forlornly.

Webb Paulson looked back. 'You got guts, I'll say that for you.' He said. 'Jump up behind Abe. *Now!*' he shouted when she hesitated.

Sarah did as she was told.

When they got back to the clearing Zeke was lying by the stream applying a wet bandanna to his throbbing head wound. As soon as he saw Sarah he leaped to his feet, then tottered. Almost falling headlong he grabbed a sapling for support. He drew his hunting knife and yelled, 'I'm gonna skin her alive.' He lurched threateningly towards her.

Webb rode his horse between them. 'Put that knife away,' he commanded. 'You deserve what she give you, for bein' stupid.'

Zeke meekly put away the knife, but his eyes were burning with hatred. Zeke wanted revenge, and he wanted it badly. Wanted to defile her young body, make her know who was boss. Only after he had his way with her would he kill her.

At that moment he loathed his

brother, realizing how much he had hated Webb all his life. He was the one Webb always picked on. Well, soon that would all change. Zeke returned to the stream and sat down.

'Pick her out another horse,' Webb said to Abe, 'then check on our wounded soldier.' He chortled, nodding towards Zeke, who was dabbing the wet bandanna to the side of his head. Webb looked at the sky. 'I want to get to the shack before dark.'

⋆   ⋆   ⋆

The Paulsons and their hostage entered a sharply curving narrow gorge that afforded some small respite from the harsh wind. The steep sides of the canyon narrowed, becoming only wide enough to allow one horse to pass at one time.

Zeke Paulson kept a tight grip on the halter of Sarah's horse, pulling her mount through the tiny space behind him. His face was full of thunder.

The tight trail continued downhill,

the gentle slope a much welcome relief after the strenuous climb in near blizzard conditions of the previous night.

The four rider procession descended from the pass, leaving the melting snowline behind. The temperature rose with every step. The area facing them was known as High Flats Pasture, a vast bowl of meadowland surrounded by high peaks, and full of low-growing brush, tall waving grass and an abundance of tough purple sage.

Clear streams ran on either side of the ever-widening game trail. A few cows gazed at the invaders of their lush meadowland. The sharp contrast in the weather here with that of Beartooth Pass was incredible.

Overhead, small puffs of white cloud drifted lazily across the cobalt-blue sky. At the far end of the pasture-land a small stone-built cabin sat prominently on a small rise, like an upturned wash-basin.

'Think that fella's still behind us?' asked Abe.

For a long moment his older brother said nothing; it was obvious that he was thinking. Abe stayed silent. He knew not to speak when Webb went into one of his contemplations, as he called them.

'You and Zeke carry on with the girl. Stay on this trail,' Webb ordered.

'What you gonna do?' asked Abe.

'I'm gonna fix that son'va bitch. Make him wish he'd kept clear of us.'

'You aimin' to shoot 'im, Webb?' Zeke piped up.

Webb Paulson gave Zeke a chilling look. 'Get goin',' he ordered, waving a hand. 'Wait for me at the line shack.' He turned his mount and rode back along the trail.

'You heard the man,' Abe called out. 'Let's go.'

* * *

The wind of a rifle bullet whipped harmlessly past his cheek. Jeff felt the searing heat as the projectile parted the air a split second before the single large-bore gunshot echoed through the rocks. A second bullet creased the side of Jeff's head; his hat flew backwards as if it had been caught by a sudden gust of wind. Behind him both bullets whined as the spent lead ricocheted from rock to rock.

Instinctively Jeff dived for cover, trying to ignore the intense pain in his head and dragging Ajax's and Atlas's reins. He urged his horses behind a large boulder and cried out loudly when his knee collided with a sharp piece of stone. For a moment he lay still as a grey mist descended, blurring his stunned vision. He let go the reins as a third shot smacked into the earth near his leg. Atlas and Ajax shied away from the gunfire, then broke into a frightened run back along the trail.

Jeff tried to haul his aching body erect, using a rock for support. He found he couldn't see, nor could he stand properly. As soon as he lifted his hand from the rock he tottered, staggering backwards towards the edge of an unseen shallow ravine.

His boot heel found nothing but air as he stepped back. His arms flailed around for something to hold on to, his fingers scraped on stone, his hands grasped at clumps of brush. He was falling, the power of gravity was too strong to resist. His forehead banged against the rock face as he half-fell, half-slid backwards. Then suddenly his body was in free fall.

Jeff's unconscious body hit the bottom of a deep cleft with a thud, knocking the wind from his lungs. Blood oozed from a gash on his forehead and from the bullet crease.

Webb Paulson looked down into the cleft, saw the blood and grinned. Whoever this guy was, he was history now. Sometimes tough lessons have to be learned. Webb chuckled to himself as he mounted his horse, proud of his skill with a rifle.

★   ★   ★

Jeff opened one eye and then the other; his vision was blurred. He blinked rapidly, scrunching up his eyes. When he opened them again he found himself staring at a jagged rock. He lifted a hand to his aching head; when he took it away and looked at it the glove was covered in blood. For a moment his confused brain wasn't able to process any of the information it was receiving about the situation its owner found himself in. His back felt as if it had been hit by a locomotive, his legs wouldn't move. He feared they were broken, and panic surged up from the pit of his stomach. He wanted to be sick.

A stabbing pain lanced his side; he knew he was hurt, but how badly, he couldn't tell. Slowly his memory of what had happened kicked in, and he began to regain the use of his limbs. He turned over on to his back; the bright sky was clear and blue.

It took a few more minutes but eventually and with great difficulty Jeff managed to push his body into a sitting position. Leaning his back against the cold hard rock face he looked up at the place he had fallen from: over twenty feet at least. It would be a difficult climb, but it was one he had to make.

Jeff reached for the first handhold, then a second one, cursing himself for being stupid enough to ride into an ambush. Bruised and sore, hand over hand Jeff hauled his weary body over the edge of the ravine.

Of his two horses there was no sign. He took off a glove, put his fingers between his lips and gave a whistle, for a moment forgetting that his bushwhacker might hear it and come back to finish the job. There was no way he could tell if the bastard was still waiting for him. Jeff cursed his stupidity a second time, but a minute later his face broke into a smile as Atlas trotted around a bend in the trail, Ajax following behind. Jeff thanked God for once again looking after him.

Jeff grabbed Atlas's trailing reins and

managed to get to his feet. A couple of times he almost fell as he rose on to his unsteady legs, testing each in turn with his full weight. Satisfied there was no lasting damage, he guided the horses to a spot behind a large boulder.

After retrieving his hat Jeff risked a quick glance around the boulder, but saw nothing.

His head and knee throbbed as if he'd been kicked by a team of mules. Tugging the horses further in behind the rocks Jeff reached for his Winchester and his telescope, glad that he'd left it looped around the saddle pommel.

He tethered the horses and scrambled up a shale-covered cut between two rocky outcrops until he was around twenty or so feet higher than where his horses waited. Through a tiny gap between two rocks he steadied the telescope, one gloved hand shielding the glass against any reflection of the sun that might give away his position. He scanned the rocks facing him for some sign of movement. All was still and quiet. He snapped the scope shut and pushed it inside his coat, then worked his way round to the place where he figured the shooter was most likely to have been hidden. Or, might still be, he thought, hoping he hadn't made a mistake; he hadn't heard any sound of hoofbeats, the shooter might still be around somewhere.

Ten minutes of painful crawling and cautious progress brought him into a shady spot covered by overhanging rock. Three large-calibre shell-casings lay discarded on the sandy ground. Jeff took off a glove and reached out a hand: the casings were still warm. He lifted one nearer his eyes: .50–.90 Sharps carbine, he figured. Looking around he found two or three large bootprints, more than one size bigger than his own. The prints were deep, made by a big heavyset man. From the descriptions the bank clerk had given this must be Webb Paulson. But where had he disappeared to?

23

The old line shack, High Flats Pasture, Absaroka Mountains

The line shack door slammed back on its hinges.

'It's blocked!' Zeke Paulson's teeth chattered as he threw his gloves on to the rough-sawn wooden table, and draped his coat over the back of one of the cabin's three chairs. He stamped his feet noisily. There was still ice and snow on his hat, and on the coat.

Webb had sent the youngest Paulson ahead to check the condition of the high pass.

Zeke's eyes focused on the piles of banknotes on the table in front of his eldest brother.

Webb's hooded look silenced Zeke's unasked question.

'You're sure?' Webb demanded gruffly.

'Sure as sure can be,' Zeke replied confidently. 'Couldn't slide a snake through. Snow's higher'n a house.' He sniffed. 'Any coffee?'

Abe poured Zeke a cup.

Webb Paulson cursed loudly. He stood, knocking over the chair. He kicked the wall closest to him, then, mid-curse, drew his hunting knife and threw it at the door in a temper. The quivering blade embedded an inch or two.

'Blast it!' Webb yelled, retrieving the knife. His mind whirred, trying to come up with a workable alternative plan. His frustration threatened to boil over into more violence and his two brothers cowered back against the wall of the cabin. Webb kicked a bucket, spilling the contents over the timber floor.

The options were severely limited and he knew it. There were only two. One: hole up in the line shack and wait for the pass to thaw, fight off anybody who came near. Two: return the way they had come, and fight off anybody they encountered on the trail. Webb cursed again, not liking either option one little bit, wishing he could get his hands on the Indian scout he'd met at Fort Ellis who told him the high pass would be open for at least another month. Maybe more, the scout had added.

'Get me some food!' he yelled to nobody and everybody. 'Any more of that rotgut left?'

Abe picked up the bottle and shook it. 'There's a whisker or two left,' he said.

'Give it here.' Webb snatched the bottle from his brother's hand. He raised it to his parched lips, drained the last of the fiery liquid, then hurled the bottle at the wall, where it shattered into tiny pieces. 'Get me some food, I said,' he bellowed.

★   ★   ★

A plume of grey smoke rose skyward above the gigantic boulders of the lower slopes of the western end of Beartooth Pass. Jeff knew immediately where it was coming from — the old line shack on High Flats Pasture. He reined in Ajax and dismounted, choosing to walk down the last part of the trail, thus concealing himself and his horses.

He rested the telescope on a rock and scanned the shack and the terrain around it. There were at least six horses in the corral, Jeff had a feeling there were more hidden from view.

Around ten minutes later a tall gangly man came out on to the porch; he was carrying a rifle. The man must have been well over six feet tall with a hard-boned, unshaven face, lean; there seemed to be no softness in him. He appeared to look directly at Jeff, but gave no sign that he had seen anything out of the ordinary. After a few minutes of staring into space the man sat down on a chair, the rifle resting easy across his legs.

Jeff's dilemma was how to get across the open ground between the end of the canyon and the line shack without being seen; there didn't appear to be much in the way of cover.

After considering his options Jeff decided to go back up the trail, make camp and wait for nightfall. He'd marked a likely spot a few hundred yards back where a small grassy clearing offered good cover and shelter. He remembered that there was a tiny flow of clean water which, even in high summer, dripped into a small pool from an overhanging rock.

The clearing was covered in ferns and verdant grass that smelled wonderful. He slackened the cinch straps on his horses and allowed them to graze.

Jeff decided to risk a small fire and brewed a pot of strong coffee whilst he waited for a pan of beans to heat up. After eating he disassembled, cleaned and oiled his weapons one by one, then reloaded them.

A plan was beginning to form in his mind. He looked up at the darkening sky; sundown would be in less than an hour, that was when he would work his way to the line shack.

The sound of hoofs thumping on the hard ground further back along the trail rumbled through the narrow canyon behind him; six or seven horses, he guessed, were coming slow and easy. He hoped it was the posse. It made sense that they would catch him up; they hadn't had to search for the tracks of the fugitives as he had, nor had they had to wait for Red Hawk and his braves.

He decided to wait and see who it was. He picked up his Winchester and took cover behind a rock.

The hoofbeats grew louder, then stopped. Jeff figured the riders were reluctant to travel much further in the growing gloom. He had to know who it was behind him, so he left the security of his place of concealment and made his way into the canyon, keeping close to the rock wall, moving cautiously through the shadows in a half-crouch.

The sound of whispering voices drifted on the wind. Round a bend in the trail, in a small clearing, eight men sat around a small fire that looked as though it had just got going. Jeff's heart leaped when he recognized the two men facing in his direction. Weak firelight reflected from his brother's face: Clem was with the posse. The second man was Jeff's deputy, Ben North.

Jeff rose up out of his crouch; his back ached painfully; almost as much as his head and side.

'Clem. Ben,' he called out softly.

In the camp hands flew to weapons, feet scraped on the earth as their owners scrambled out of the firelight.

'Clem. Ben,' Jeff repeated. 'It's Jeff.' He walked unsteadily into the open, his aching knee threatening to collapse with each step. 'Don't shoot,' he thought to add.

'Jeff?' Clem answered. 'That you?'

'It's me,' said Jeff, stepping into the firelight.

Clem pushed away his bedroll and scrambled to his feet. He hurried across the open ground between him and his brother as fast as he could. He clasped Jeff's hand, then gave him a hug.

'Good to see you,' he said warmly.

For the briefest moment Jeff was overcome with the relief of unexpectedly seeing his younger brother with the posse. Emotion filled his throat, making it difficult to speak.

Clem spoke first. 'Soon as I heard what had happened I saddled up an' chased after Ben here.' He grinned. 'Figured he could use an extra gun.'

Jeff found his unsteady voice. 'I'm glad to see you,' he said. 'All of you,' he added, sweeping his hand in a wide arc.

'Coffee's brewing,' Ben called out. 'Help keep out the chill.'

'Be mighty welcome,' said Jeff. He followed his brother to the fire.

The other members of the posse called out their own greetings, each of which Jeff acknowledged individually. He sat crossed-legged, warming his cold hands on the glowing embers and gave a report on what had happened. Clem noticed the dried blood on his brother's face. Jeff explained the ambush and how he had fallen into the ravine. When he had finished his story, Jeff announced he wanted to get his horses. Clem went with him.

The two brothers were back with the posse in no time. More coffee followed a plate of hot food.

Ben contemplated the new developments. 'So what we need is a plan to get Sarah back safe and sound an' in one piece.' Ben realized he was stating the obvious.

Jeff listened to the chatter that followed: just that of a regular bunch of cowpokes around a campfire. He found the company heart-warming and welcome after his lonely pursuit of the bank robbers.

A member of the posse made a suggestion. 'Why not run off their horses?'

'Maybe we will,' Jeff answered, 'but first we need to make certain Sarah is all right. And,' he added, 'we need to make sure there's only three of them.'

'Only three of 'em got away?' Ben queried.

'Yes, but there may have been others

waiting for them,' Jeff suggested.

Ben held up a hand. 'Hadn't thought of that.'

'This is how I see it,' Jeff said. 'After sundown I'll work my way to the line shack. See if I can see Sarah and see how she's being treated. That'll determine how best to proceed.'

'You think they may have hurt her?' asked one of the posse.

'No idea,' Jeff replied. 'I just hope not.' He looked at his watch, 'I'll move out in half an hour or so.'

'I'm coming with you,' Clem announced.

Jeff nodded, happy at the prospect of having his brother's company.

★　★　★

It was almost pitch dark when Jeff and Clem set off on foot down the trail. Black clouds filled the sky; there was no silvery moon to help guide their footfall. The two men toted Winchesters in gloved hands, their hats were pulled low, their coat collars turned up against the chill. The tall grass and purple sage made a pattern of dark patches dotted across the landscape.

On reaching the edge of the pasture the two brothers removed their spurs so as not to make any unnecessary give-away sounds. 'No need to advertise our presence,' Jeff had said, laying his on the ground against a large flat boulder from where they could be retrieved later.

The grass was wet with dew and in seconds the front of their clothing was soaked. Jeff pushed the Winchester ahead as he inched forward on his belly. The pain in his knee stabbed each time he put any weight on it; this journey was going to take some time, but Clem was a reassuring presence behind him. The dark night closed tightly around them.

Jeff figured it was still about fifty yards to the line shack when suddenly a light appeared at a window, casting a shaft of yellow on the earth; the tall man with the rifle had disappeared. Jeff looked back at his brother, Clem's face showed pale against the grey landscape. Jeff made a sign for Clem to veer off to the right and to halt a few yards from the shack. Clem nodded his understanding and moved away silently; it was like being back in the war.

Jeff glanced over his shoulder; his brother was nowhere to be seen, only the ghostly outline of the grass waving gently in the chill breeze. At the corner of the corral he paused to look around. There were horses there, he could hear their snorting and breathing, and could just about make out the dark outline of their shapes, but couldn't see how many there were.

He reached out a hand to take hold of a cross-rail, feeling the wood, cold and rough on his skin. He hauled himself more erect in order to get a better view. As he leant against a fence post Jeff felt the presence of a horse, then felt a nudge on his shoulder. Startled, he flinched away, his hand sweeping down to the six-gun at his side. The animal snorted, and pushed its head over the top cross-rail. Jeff smiled to himself at his frightened reaction, he stroked the horse's nose, then dropped down into a crouch.

Soundlessly he felt his way along the corral fence; the outline of the line shack showed dark against the ever-lightening sky. Without making the slightest whisper of sound Jeff crossed the open space between the corral and the shack in a few long stealthy strides, keeping as low as he could.

Resting his back against the timber wall of the line shack, his head to one side, he held his breath and listened. The loudest noise was the rhythmic beating of his own heart. Then another sound, reminiscent of a large pig, pierced the chill air.

In one silent movement Jeff was at the window. He removed his hat and peered into the room. One bareheaded man sat at a table playing solitaire; a single lantern at his elbow cast eerie shadows on the walls. He was big and heavyset with an unkempt black beard and thinning hair. His expression seemed to be one of a constant sneer. A pair of six-guns lay on the table near enough for the man to reach in a hurry; on the other side of the table were large piles of green banknotes.

The big man raised his head abruptly to look directly at the window. Jeff ducked down quickly, holding his breath, not daring to make a sound, hoping he had not been seen. He drew the Remington, his hand trembling slightly, and waited for what seemed like an age, but was in fact only a few seconds. When no other sound came he risked another quick peek through the window. The man at the table had returned to his game.

Suddenly the man shouted an expletive, threw down the cards irritatedly, then scraped them together into a pack. He shuffled them repeatedly then dealt again. For a moment Jeff had been concerned in case the man's actions had signalled something he should fear, but obviously the cards hadn't been falling as the man hoped.

Jeff eased his body to stand more erect so that he could scan more of the shack's interior. Against the far wall he saw a bunk and on it the dark shape of a man. Jeff saw whiskers; their owner was making a good deal of noise. The woollen blanket covering the shape rose and fell in time with the loud snoring.

In one sudden movement the big man rose from his chair, tossed the pack of cards on to the table, then crossed the room and aimed a kick at the bunk. The snoring ceased abruptly as the shape snuffled, then sat up.

Rubbing his eyes Zeke looked up at his brother.

'Whatdya do that for?' Zeke called out.

'To shut you up,' the big man growled.

Zeke hawked up a mouthful and looked around for somewhere to deposit the contents of his mouth. Seeing nothing suitable he spat on the floor.

Webb pushed Zeke heavily on the

shoulder. 'Clean that up,' he said menac-
ingly.

Zeke Paulson untied the bandanna
from around his neck and wiped up the
offending deposit, leaving only a damp
stain on the wooden floorboard.

'Anythin' to drink?' he asked.

'On the table,' the big man replied.
He saw where Zeke's piggy eyes went.
'Get it yourself,' he added venomously.

Jeff watched the man get up from the
bunk and lurch across the room. That
was when he saw Sarah. She raised
herself into a sitting position, leaning
her back against the wall of the shack,
her legs bent, knees under her chin. Her
eyes were closed, her tied wrists were
resting on her knees. Jeff couldn't see
much of her face, but from what he
could see she looked forlorn and
without hope. He hadn't been able to
see her before because she had been
hidden behind the sleeping man.

The big man leaned closer to Sarah,
he inspected her hands. Satisfied, he
returned to the table, pausing briefly to

poke some life back into the dim fire burning in the fireplace. Jeff could smell the stewed coffee inside the pot that stood on the hearth; he could almost taste it.

Webb Paulson reached the table, a broad grin across his face, just as Zeke raised the bottle of spirits to his thick lips. The bottle fell on to the wooden floorboards with a dull thud, but didn't break.

'It's empty,' Zeke complained. 'There's nothing in there.' He saw his older brother's expression. 'You knew it, didn't you?' he yelled.

Webb let out a loud guffaw. 'Hell yes. I drank it all,' he admitted.

The sound of the bottle hitting the floor drew Sarah's attention. Jeff saw how drawn and strained she looked. Her dull dark eyes, normally sparkling, held a fear she couldn't hide. She sat stock still, as though afraid to move.

Zeke's hand covered the banknote on the top of one pile.

'Leave that!' Webb warned.

Zeke withdrew his hand quickly. 'Where's Abe?' he asked.

'Out lookin' at the horses.' Webb answered.

Sarah spoke, her voice tiny and wavering. 'Can I have a drink of water, please?'

Webb Paulson turned his head to look in her direction.

'Water,' she repeated shakily. 'Can I have some?'

'Canteen's over there.' His head nodded towards the water canteen hanging from a hook on the wall near the fireplace.

Jeff had seen enough. The outline of a plan had formed clearly in his head. He was about to make his way back to Ben and the posse when he heard a loud scuffling coming from the front of the shack. Sarah heard it too. It stopped her in her tracks as she reached her tied hands towards the canteen of water.

Webb and Zeke Paulson also heard the sound. The pair exchanged concerned looks. Webb got up from the table, lit another lantern and crossed to the door. He opened it and called out into the darkness, 'Abe! You OK?'

For a moment only silence came back, then a muffled voice said, 'Yeah.'

Webb stepped out on to the stoop at the front of the shack. A pool of light from the lantern cast shadowy shapes. In the corral horses milled about, snorting and snuffling.

As he stood by the corner of the shack Jeff wondered what had happened. Had Abe seen Clem? He peered at Webb Paulson, feeling the need to take some kind of action, seeing his plan going out of the window.

Zeke Paulson appeared at his brother's shoulder. 'What's he gone an' done?'

'Get back inside,' Webb snarled. 'Watch the girl.'

Disappointed, Zeke turned on his heel, his face colliding with the heavy skillet that Sarah swung two-handed with all the strength she could muster. Blood spurted as the iron pan smashed Zeke's nose.

Sarah had seen her chance to escape and had taken it without hesitation.

Webb swung round in time to see Zeke flop to the floor like a sack of potatoes.

Jeff hadn't planned it this way, but Sarah's actions made up his mind for him. In two long strides he was on the stoop. Holding his Remington by the barrel he crash dived on to Webb Paulson, knocking the big man off balance, at the same time bringing the butt of the six-gun down with all his power. The makeshift club missed its mark, bouncing off Webb's shoulder.

Instinctively Webb arched his body like an unbroken bronc, bucking Jeff over his shoulder; the momentum of Jeff's dive helped the throw. Jeff landed on top of Zeke's prostrate body. He tried to right himself but Webb smashed a savage right-hander into his cheek. For a split second the lights threatened to go out, such was the force Webb put into the punch.

Webb Paulson cursed loudly; his Colts

remained where he'd left them, on the table. He grabbed the bone-handled hunting knife from the scabbard on his belt and threw himself forward, arm raised ready to bring the knife down.

Jeff struggled to get his gun up so he could fire, as Sarah hurled the skillet at Webb Paulson. The knife clattered into a corner of the room. Webb snarled and dived at Jeff who managed to roll away sideways, in the process banging his hand on the leg of the table. The Remington spun out of his grip.

Outside, moments earlier, Clem made for the shack, but Abe Paulson grabbed hold of his leg. Clem's head hit the edge of the stoop as he fell forward, dazing him, but not knocking him out. In an instant Abe was on him, blood streaming down his face into his eyes from the deep gash on his forehead.

Abe went for his gun but, even as the Colt came up, Clem swung the spade he'd picked up. The sharp edge buried itself in Abe's forehead. Abe's Colt fell harmlessly to the hard earth. The semi-dazed pair rolled around, neither able to deliver a clean punch at the other.

Inside the shack Webb Paulson struggled to his feet. Sarah jumped at him, her fingers clawed at his eyes. Webb pushed her away roughly: his huge fist, colliding with her nose, knocked her backwards against the wall of the shack.

Zeke recovered sufficiently to make a grab for Jeff's leg. Jeff silenced him with a swift kick to the head. His boot heels scrambled to push his body clear of the giant facing him.

Webb's darting eyes went to the six-guns on the table. Jeff saw where he was looking. Webb dived for the Colts at the same time as Jeff's hand lit upon the Remington. Two hammers clicked back loudly. Two loud explosions echoed around the interior of the line shack. The air was filled with acrid gunsmoke.

Webb Paulson had always been good with a gun, so good that he expected to beat any man he went up against. After all, he had killed more than his fair share of would-be gunslingers and lawmen in his time. He stood stock still, staring at his adversary for a split second, his still smoking Colt in his hand.

Webb's expression changed from confident determination to surprise. The Colt slipped from his fingers, his knees buckled under him and he fell forward to the floor.

Jeff reached out his left hand, grabbed the edge of the table, and hauled his aching body erect. The smoking Remington in his right hand had again done its job. Jeff's bullet had smashed through Webb Paulson's heart.

Jeff brushed a hand across his cheek, feeling a stinging pain where Webb Paulson's bullet had skimmed the skin. He took his hand away and looked down, there was blood on it. In the corner Sarah whimpered as she recovered consciousness. Jeff looked at her, there was blood on her lip and nose, a large bruise was forming on her cheek.

The sound of boots on wood caused

Jeff to spin round. The tall figure of Abe Paulson stood in the open doorway, silhouetted against the first streaks of red and gold in the sky. His face was a mask of blood, Winchester in hand.

Jeff fired; in his mind there was no time for any other action.

Abe turned his head to look where the shot had come from as the rifle dropped to the floor. It was now obvious he had been half-blinded by his own blood.

Abe Paulson's lifeless body slumped to the floor as Clem reached the doorway, six-gun in hand. A trickle of blood flowed from the side of his temple. He looked down at the prone bodies of the Paulson brothers then at his own brother.

'Sorry,' he said, his voice wavering.

Jeff holstered the Remington and moved to the doorway. He reached down and yanked Zeke's arms behind his back. He lifted the handcuffs from the back of his gunbelt and slapped the cuffs on Zeke's wrists.

'Not exactly what we had planned, eh?' he said to his brother.

Clem smiled weakly. 'You can sure say that again,' he said. Clem leaned against the doorframe.

Jeff picked up Webb's hunting knife and slit Sarah's bonds. She looked up into the face of her rescuer.

'Thank you,' she said.

'No,' said Jeff. 'Thank *you*. Couldn't have done it without you.' He held out a hand to her. She took it. She rose to her feet and moved to embrace Jeff.

Sarah was the image of her mother. In the five years he had known her Jeff had watched her grow from child through adolescence into the beautiful young woman she was today.

Clem managed to stagger to the table, he sat down heavily as the sound of galloping horses drifted across the pastureland.

Jeff shouted as horses drew up outside. 'Everything's OK!'

Deputy Ben North stepped across the threshold gripping a Colt .45 tightly in his hand. His eyes took in the bloody spectacle before him; instantly he knew what scene had been played out in the small room.

'We came as soon as we heard shooting,' he said, shaking Jeff's hand.

The bodies of Webb and Abe Paulson were wrapped in blankets, draped across the backs of a couple of horses and tied on securely. Zeke Paulson recovered consciousness and loudly protested his innocence, complaining about everything and nothing, swearing that his two older brothers had forced him into joining them on the bank raid. No one took the slightest notice of him.

The stolen money was recovered in full, spare horses were roped together, and the posse set off to return to White Bluff. Thankfully the harsh weather had eased considerably, making for an easy trek through Beartooth Pass.

At Three Forks Canyon Jeff and the posse met up with Red Hawk and his band of Crow warriors. Ika and Jason were with them.

A tear formed in the corner of Jeff's eye as he witnessed the emotional reunion.

Ika rode her pony next to Atlas, her leg almost touching Jeff's. She thanked him, touched his hand, then spurred her pony away to join Red Hawk and his Crow braves.

Along with Sarah and Jason, she paused a few yards inside the canyon. All three turned and waved. Jeff raised an arm and waved back, knowing he wouldn't see Ika again for a long time.

Clem kicked his horse forward alongside Jeff's horse and touched his brother's arm. He seemed to sense what was happening.

Jeff nodded as Clem spoke. 'All worked out fine,' he observed. 'Sarah's back safe, bank money's recovered. Two *bandidos* are dead, the other in custody. Ain't had this much excitement in years.' He rubbed his temple.

Jeff smiled, but inside he felt that a part of him had died. He turned Atlas's head towards White Bluff, and led the happy posse back home. He contemplated all that had happened and considered the future with every jolting step of his horse.

As he led the way along Main Street he reached the decision he had wrestled with for many miles.

His life was with Laurie and the boys; Ika had been right about that. Jeff owed it to Laurie and to the twins to spend the rest of his life making them happy. He would resign his position as sheriff and would take Laurie on a trip back East. They would call in at Evansville on the way to leave Josh and Joel with his mother and father.

The weary posse reined in outside the jail and dismounted. Jeff stayed in the saddle. He called Ben to him, plucked the tin star from his chest and handed it over. He told his deputy what was in his mind.

Doctor Hollis walked across the street accompanied by two other members of the town council.

'I'll need to take a look at your

wounds,' he said, seeing the blood-stains.

'Come over to my house later,' Jeff told him. 'I probably look worse than I feel. Anyhow I've got something urgent to tell Laurie and it won't wait.'

Jeff announced his plans and his irreversible decision, together with his recommendation that the job of sheriff be given to Ben North. The councillors reluctantly accepted Jeff's decision with sadness but understanding.

Considerably relieved Jeff rode home. He felt better and happier than at any time in the past few weeks.

The door opened wide and a smiling Laurie stepped through. Jeff swung an aching leg over Atlas's back and stepped down. He smiled warmly at his wife as he hitched his horse to the rail.

When she saw the bloodstains Laurie's hand flew to her mouth, the other she pressed against her chest. Her expectant eyes were red-rimmed from all the crying she had done since Jeff's departure.

'It's nothing,' Jeff told her.

Her husband's face betrayed none of the anxiety that he had felt the night before he had left. Dared she hope for an improvement in their relationship?

She took a step forward as her husband climbed the steps to the front porch. Jeff took off his hat and threw it on to one of the two easy chairs on the porch under the window. He held out both arms to her.

Laurie needed no second invitation. She rushed forward and felt Jeff's powerful arms enfold her. He hugged her to him; she snuggled her head against his chest.

Keeping one arm around her Jeff lifted her chin with his free hand and kissed her forehead, her nose, and cheeks in turn. The best and most passionate kiss he reserved for her lips.

Blissfully Laurie felt all the love that Jeff put into that long kiss. He kissed her again. It was as though the past few weeks had been a dream.

'I probably stink,' he said abruptly, breaking off from their kissing. 'Let me get a quick wash and some clean duds, then we'll get something to eat. I'm starving.'

'I have nothing prepared,' Laurie apologized. 'I didn't know when to expec — '

Jeff halted her unnecessary excuses with a finger on her lips. 'We'll go to Ma O'Shaughnessy's,' he told her. 'Your dad can look after the boys.'

Laurie's eyes sparkled for the first time in ages. 'What's happened?' she asked.

'I'll tell you everything while I get cleaned up,' said Jeff, 'but I will tell you one thing now.' Her expectant eyes held his. 'I have resigned as sheriff. And you, young lady, are going on a special trip back East.'

Laurie screamed with delight.

THE END

We do hope that you have enjoyed reading this large print book.

Did you know that all of our titles are available for purchase?

We publish a wide range of high quality large print books including:
Romances, Mysteries, Classics General Fiction Non Fiction and Westerns

Special interest titles available in large print are:
The Little Oxford Dictionary Music Book, Song Book Hymn Book, Service Book

Also available from us courtesy of Oxford University Press:
Young Readers' Dictionary (large print edition) Young Readers' Thesaurus (large print edition)

For further information or a free brochure, please contact us at:
Ulverscroft Large Print Books Ltd., The Green, Bradgate Road, Anstey, Leicester, LE7 7FU, England. Tel: (00 44) **0116 236 4325 Fax:** (00 44) **0116 234 0205**

Other titles in the
Linford Western Library:

DUEL OF THE OUTLAWS

John Russell Fearn

The inhabitants of Twin Pines, Arizona lead uneventful, happy lives — until the sudden arrival of Black Yankee and his gang. They shoot the sheriff, take over the place, and Twin Pines spirals downwards into an outlaw town, with lawlessness and sudden death the norm. When Thorn Tanworth, son of the sheriff, returns from his travels, to everyone's astonishment he establishes a mutually beneficial partnership with Black Yankee. But then the two men begin fighting each other for control of the town . . .

KID FURY

Michael D. George

The remote settlement of War Smoke lies quiet — until the calm is shattered by a gunshot. Marshal Matt Fallen and his deputy Elmer spring into action to investigate. Then another shot rings out, and cowboy Billy Jackson's horse gallops into town, dragging its owner's corpse in the dust: one boot still caught in its stirrup, and one hand gripping a smoking gun. Meanwhile, the paths of hired killer Waco Walt Dando and gunfighter Kid Fury are set to converge on War Smoke . . .

FIVE SHOTS LEFT

Ben Bridges

When you have only five shots left, you have to make each one count. Like the outlaw whose quest for revenge didn't go quite according to plan. Or the cowboy who ended up using a most unusual weapon to defeat his enemy. Then there was the store-keeper who had to face his worst fear. A down-at-heel sheepherder who was obliged to set past hatreds aside when renegade Comanches went on the warpath. And an elderly couple who struggled to keep the secret that threatened to tear them apart . . .

VENGEANCE TRAIL

Steve Hayes

A vengeance trail brings Waco McAllum to Santa Rosa, hunting his brother's killers: a grudge which can only be settled by blood. He finds valuable allies in Drifter, Latigo Rawlins, and Gabriel Moonlight — three men who are no strangers to trouble. But along the way, he finds himself on another trail: a crooked one that leads straight to a gang of violent cattle-rustlers. In the final showdown, will Waco get his revenge — or a whole lot more besides?

A ROPE FOR IRON EYES

Rory Black

Notorious bounty hunter Iron Eyes corners the deadly Brand brothers in the house with the red lamp above its door. As the outlaws enjoy themselves, Iron Eyes bursts in with guns blazing. But Matt Brand and his siblings are harder to kill than most wanted men: they fight like tigers, and Iron Eyes is lynched before they ride off. Yet even a rope cannot stop Iron Eyes. And he is determined to resume his deadly hunt, regardless of whoever dares stand in his way.